BUCK and the BLUE ROAN

Stormy Kurtz

SOUL FIRE PRESS

an imprint of
Christopher Matthews Publishing

Boston, Massachusetts

Buck and the Blue Roan

Copyright © 2017 by Stormy Kurtz

All rights reserved. Except as permitted under the U.S. Copyright Act of 1976, no part of this publication may be reproduced, distributed or transmitted in any form or by any means, or stored in a database or retrieval system without the prior written permission of the author. All characters appearing in this work are fictitious. Any resemblance to persons, living or dead, is purely coincidental.

Editors: Jeremy Soldevilla
Cover design: MJC Imageworks

ISBN 978-1-948146-22-0
ebook ISBN 978-1-945146-23-7

Published by
Soul Fire Press

an imprint of
CHRISTOPHER MATTHEWS PUBLISHING
Boston
Printed in the United States of America

Acknowledgments

I wish to thank my family and many friends who encouraged me along the way with this story. I want to thank Ric Rodolph, who passed away in July 2016. His editorial comments and sense of humor brought life to many scenes. I also want to thank Tyler Harrington for his editorial comments regarding the language of his generation. I especially want to thank my husband, Ron, whose unflagging love and support have enabled me to stay focused on this project. Finally, I want to thank my editor, Jeremy Soldevilla, for his wise counsel and encouragement.

Contents

Broken Promises 1
At Magruder's Corral 11
Elvira 25
My Friends Call Me Ellie 46
Ornery Bronc 60
Point of No Return 71
Sold 83
Headin' and Heelin' 98
Black Widow 112
Hell Hath No Fury 129
Missing Saddles 143
Dumped Again 156
Thou Shalt Not Steal 169
Spirit Helper 183
To Catch a Thief 197
Buck Evens the Score 211
Closing the Circle 227
About the Author 237

Broken Promises

BUCK EAGLE PLUME HUNCHED his shoulders against the raw March wind blowing across the Flathead Valley. He squinted his eyes to protect them from the sting, but they watered anyway. On the Flathead reservation, spring teased the snow into a soupy mixture of mud and manure, but the Mission Mountains across the valley stood tall, still frozen and forbidding beneath tons of snow, silent sentinels against the gray Montana sky. Buck shuffled his cold feet and wiggled his toes, hoping the friction would restore some warmth. He wished he could be anywhere but here in the barnyard of his grandfather's small ranch. Even his Senior English class at St. Ignatius High School would be a welcome relief. He looked at his watch and pictured his friends sitting in class, yawning, while Mrs. Baines tried to convince them of the life-changing importance of learning to diagram sentences. If only it was summer . . .

"Buck . . . Buck? Hey, are you okay?"

The veterinarian's voice jarred Buck back to the present. "Yah, I'm fine. What next?"

"I'll try another injection of Rompun. It's the strongest pain drug I can use. If he doesn't respond to this, I'm afraid we'll lose him."

Buck watched as the veterinarian leaned over the trembling horse and slipped the hypodermic needle into the animal's jugular vein. The buckskin gelding lay on the ground, shaking from deep shock, his caramel-colored coat blotched with sweat and mud.

"Okay, try to get him on his feet. "The veterinarian stepped back to get out of the way.

Buck pulled on the lead rope. "Come on, Chester, get up. Come on, boy, try!"

The gelding lifted his head and groaned, but made no attempt to rise. The vet kneeled down and felt for the pulse under the horse's lower jaw. Then he lifted the upper lip and pressed his thumb to the gray-white gums. He turned to Buck and put his hand on the young man's shoulder. "I'm sorry. There's no change in his vital signs. This is the worst kind of colic a horse can get. Everything points to a twisted gut. The best thing you can do for him now is to put him down."

"Doc, what about surgery? Can't you do surgery on him?" A desperate pleading softened the intensity of Buck's brown eyes.

"Buck, even if we could get him to Missoula, he probably wouldn't survive the trip. He would suffer immensely, and the bottom line is you're looking at around a two-thousand-dollar bill with no guarantee. I can't recommend surgery, but I'll try it if that's what you really want to do." The vet turned away, unable to look into Buck's anguished dark eyes any longer.

It always seemed to come down to this, money and the lack of it. How could he put a monetary value on the life of a friend? His horse was part of him; they were both part of the eternal circle of life. Now he was being asked to break the circle because he couldn't afford to pay for the possible life-saving surgery. The non-Native world was a crazy world, and Buck felt himself drowning in it. He wanted to make someone hurt the way he was hurting. All his life his father had told him that things always worked out for the best. Well, if this was the best, he didn't want anything to do with it. Maybe his mother had found a better solution after all. Buck gritted his teeth and blinked back his tears.

"Okay, Doc, put him down."

The vet returned to his truck for the lethal injection. Buck kneeled next to his gelding and stroked the powerful, sweat-drenched neck. "It'll be over soon, brother. No more pain; no more bumpy rides in the trailer; no more long days in dusty arenas; no more . . ." For a moment Buck let his tears fall on the horse's quivering neck. Then he angrily brushed them away. He was eighteen now, a man, and he had a man's job to do.

All too soon, the vet returned to his side. He spoke quietly. "I need you to pull on the lead rope to straighten his neck."

Buck moved mechanically to the gelding's head and took the rope. Once again the vet sought and found the horse's jugular. As the needle entered the vein, the vet quickly depressed the plunger. A brief shudder ran through the horse's body as the overdose of anesthetic took effect and body functions swiftly came to a halt. A few seconds later the vet pronounced the horse dead.

"I'm sorry, Buck. I know how much Chester meant to you."

"Thanks, Doc. There'll never be another team ropin' horse like him. Never!"

Buck shook hands with the vet and watched him drive down the driveway. He turned back to the dead horse and kneeled at its head. A small drop of blood trickled from the horse's nostril. Buck touched it with his fingertips, then drew them slowly across his cheeks. He raised his hands to the sky and prayed to Grandfather and the Four Directions. Finally, he leaned down and closed the horse's eyes.

"We'll bury you down by the trees, fella. You deserve better than to be coyote bait." Buck wiped his eyes again and turned away.

He walked slowly from the barn back in the direction of the ranch house. It wasn't much to look at on a sunny day, but today it looked even more drab than usual. Built in the early 1900s, it had been in Buck's family for a long time, it and the hundred and sixty acres that were part of an old government allotment given to each Native American family on the reservation. The gray, weathered boards begged for a new coat of paint, and sections of the shingles were covered with moss, indicating the rot beneath. Buck looked at the aging building and sighed. Money again. He fought momentarily with the old doorknob before it gave and let him in.

Buck didn't realize how cold he was until he got inside. He peeled off his coat and goose down vest and hung them on the coat rack his grandfather had welded using old worn-out horseshoes. He opened the firebox in the wood stove to see if it needed more wood. Red embers glowed up at him. He stirred them with an old iron poker and added another piece of wood. Steam drifted lazily from the teapot on the back lid. Buck took down a package of instant hot chocolate mix from the cupboard and put it in an old blue mug with a chipped rim. As he poured the hot water over the powdered chocolate, he breathed in the sweet steam.

"Eh oh, Bu. Me sm too?"

Buck looked up as his older brother, Rusty, shuffled into the kitchen. Buck smiled around the pain aching in his heart. "Hi, Rusty. Sure. You can have some, too. Where's Miss Hextall? You didn't lock her in the basement again, did you?"

Rusty grinned, and his eyes sparkled with mischief. "No, Bu, me no do at."

Buck knew better. Miss Hextall, the nursing aide provided by Social Services, often showed her rookie status. Rusty, a great trickster, delighted in locking her in the basement every time she went down to get food items from the pantry. She never seemed to figure out how to get around this problem. Buck fixed another mug of hot chocolate and set it on the faded, red-and-white checkered plastic cloth that covered the kitchen table.

His brother smiled up at him with child-like appreciation. "Anks, Bu."

Again, bitter tears threatened to overflow Buck's eyes. Was Rusty another example of his father's best? Was it for the best that his mother stayed drunk the whole time she carried his older brother while his father was off playing warrior chief in the military? Buck loved Rusty, but he couldn't help wondering what it would have been like if Rusty hadn't been born physically and mentally disabled. Would they have been team roping together, hunting together and dancing at pow-wows together?

"Eh, Bu, ide Chester? Wan ide, Bu."

Buck couldn't face his brother. "No, Rusty, not today."

"Ai? Wan ide, Bu. Wan ide!"

"I said, no, so knock it off!" Buck saw the hurt look on Rusty's face, but his own anger and hurt overpowered his compassion for his brother. He walked out of the small kitchen and into the hallway by the bathroom, unlocking the basement door as he went by, and, entering the living room, slouched down in the old overstuffed chair in front of the fireplace. He heard a weak, "Thanks, Buck," from Miss Hextall and then her gentle voice chiding Rusty in the kitchen for his "naughty" behavior before he dozed off.

The sound of Miss Hextall and Rusty starting dinner brought Buck back to the present. He looked at the big clock above the fireplace. It was almost five-thirty. His grandfather would be coming home soon from his job at the hospital in Missoula where he worked as an aide in physical therapy with Vietnam Vets. Buck wanted to get the chores done before his grandfather's return. He hated the idea of breaking the news about Chester. His grandfather had gone into debt to pay for the horse, and a lot of dreams had been riding on the animal's strong back. Also, with Chester had come an unspoken promise from his grandfather that he would always be there for him. Buck sensed that the gift of the horse had been his grandfather's way of trying to make up for the death of Buck's parents. Reluctantly, Buck pushed himself out of the depths of the friendly, old chair and headed for the kitchen. He avoided looking at Rusty when he passed through the kitchen to grab his coat and go outside. Usually, he took his brother with him to do chores because Rusty loved the animals so much, but tonight he didn't have the patience.

Once outside, Buck rushed through the chores, throwing hay to the two remaining horses and the steer calves. He didn't stop to visit with the stock as he usually did. Even the milk cow was treated with an unaccustomed brisk roughness. Buck took the milking stool from the peg on the wall and clanged the bucket down angrily under her udders. As he milked, he fought back the mist that blurred his vision. Buck pushed his head hard against the cow's flank and swore through clenched teeth. "Damn!"

The old Jersey cow turned and looked at him with soft, questioning eyes, but Buck ignored her. He was just finishing milking when he heard his grandfather's pickup pull in the driveway. Buck quickly threw the cow some hay, shut off the barn lights and headed for the house; warm, steaming milk sloshed from the bucket he was carrying with each step he took.

For the first time in his life, the path leading to the back door seemed too short. He drew a deep breath and braced himself for the unpleasant job ahead. He wanted nothing more than to run away from this nightmare; instead, he entered the house quietly because he knew his grandfather would be settled comfortably in the big chair by the fire.

Buck looked around for Rusty and sighed in relief when he didn't see him. Usually, Miss Hextall left as soon as his grandfather got home. He hoped Rusty didn't have her locked in the basement again, but he was glad for the solitude. This was going to be tough enough controlling his feelings without having to deal with his brother at the same time. Buck saw his grandfather's head resting against the back of the chair, and he knew his eyes would be closed because the old chair had that effect on anyone who sat in it.

The sound of the back door closing brought Ed Eagle Plume out of his semi-sleep. He sat up and rubbed his eyes as Buck walked into the living room. "Hi, Buck. I'm getting as bad as an old dog. Put me in front of a fire, and I go to sleep." The broad grin left his face when he saw his grandson's haggard expression.

Buck sagged wearily into a chair facing his grandfather. He breathed in deeply and cleared his throat. "Grandfather, I'm afraid I have some bad news."

Ed sat forward in the old chair, a difficult task considering its depth. "What's happened?"

"We lost Chester today."

"What? How?"

"He went down with colic after lunch. Miss Hextall called me home from school when she noticed him thrashing around in the corral. She didn't want to bother you at work. At first, I thought it was a simple gas colic, but walking him didn't help. He just got worse, until I couldn't even get him on his feet. Doc came out, and we worked on him for an hour. There was nothing we could do to ease his pain. Doc figured he had a twisted gut. We put him down as soon as we were sure there was no hope of saving him."

Buck swallowed hard, trying to gain control of the bile rising in his throat.

He saw the muscles tighten across his grandfather's jaw, and his Adam's apple bob as he swallowed hard, then his grandfather's body straightened in the chair as if to brace himself. The curtain closed on his emotions. He spoke in an even tone. "You made the right decision. There's no sense lettin' an animal suffer."

Buck waited for more, but it didn't come. Finally, he broke the silence. "Grandpa, I felt so helpless. We tried everything to save him."

His grandfather just stared at the fire, its orange flames dancing in the obsidian depths of his eyes. Buck's frustration mounted. He continued. "You keep tellin' me it's all going to work out for the best, that the broken circle will always be healed. How does Chester's dyin' work for the best? Where's the healing in all of this?"

Again Buck waited for his grandfather to say something. When he didn't respond, Buck's frustration pushed him beyond good judgment. "Maybe Mom was right."

A cold light came into Ed Eagle Plume's black eyes. "Don't you dare bring your mother into this conversation. You dishonor her memory."

"What are you afraid of, Grandfather? There's worse things in life than death. You of all people should know that."

Ed slammed his fist down on the arm of the old chair. A little puff of dust rose as he leaned forward, his face expressionless and his voice as cold as the March wind whipping the aging house outside. "Your mother had no control over the choices she made. You do. Don't use her as an excuse."

Buck winced under his grandfather's biting words, and he clenched his jaw to stifle the sob rising in his throat. He got up from the chair and started to walk out of the living room, hoping his grandfather's voice would call him back before he'd gone too far, but the room remained silent except for the occasional pop and hiss of the burning logs in the fireplace.

At Magruder's Corral

BEN MAGRUDER, a tall, large-framed man in his late fifties, leaned on the corral rail, watching the milling horses. Lean from years of hard work, and with thinning gray hair, he represented what was best about ranch people. Quick to laugh and slow to anger, he had a reputation among his neighbors as someone whom they could count on both in good times and bad.

The Magruder family had been ranchers in the Bitterroot valley longer than most folks could remember. Ben ran a large cow-calf operation with three hundred cows, but his real love was his horses. He looked forward to bringing in the three-year-olds to start their training under saddle. Calving and spring branding were done, and it would be several weeks before the wet earth dried up, and the irrigation pipes started pumping water to the hay fields. Ben figured tomorrow would be a good day to bring the young horses in from their mountain pasture. Satisfied with his decision, he turned away from the corrals and headed back to the house.

Ben cooked a simple dinner of steak and beans, then he prepared to go to bed. Ben's wife had died several years earlier from cancer, and they had no children. Sometimes the sprawling ranch house echoed like an empty tomb. Normally, he spent most of his evenings alone reading *The Montana Stockgrower* or entering cattle statistics into his computer, but this evening he wanted to get to bed early. The cold mornings were starting to tell on his joints, and he tired more easily after a long day in the saddle. However, before he went to bed, he made a phone call to his neighbor and closest friend, Gordon Ritter.

"Hello, Gordon. Say, tomorrow we're going to round up the three-year-olds. Would you like to join us?"

There was a short pause on the other end of the line. Ben knew Gordon would be repositioning his ever-present chew of snuff in his mouth before he gave his answer. Finally, a reply came, and Ben grinned.

"Thanks, Gordon. We'll try to get out of here around six. Bring Big Shot. It's going to be rough keepin' up with those youngsters, so you'll need a horse with savvy under you. I'll have the coffee pot on." Ben hung up the receiver with a sigh of relief. It was always good to have Gordon along. He was a top hand with a horse and a rope.

Gordon and Ben had been best friends since grade school. They'd played high school football and basketball together, been best man at each other's weddings and buried their dead together. When Ben's wife died, it was Gordon who sat up with him all night long talking and crying.

Their ranches shared a common boundary, as did their lives.

The next morning, the alarm buzzed like an angry bee. Ben groped for the clock, knocking several magazines off the nightstand before he finally found the source and silenced it with a heavy hand. He swung his legs over the edge of the bed, his feet searching for his boots. He lifted the back of his hand to his cold nose and rubbed it tentatively. The chill air caressed the back of his neck, sending a shiver through his body. He groaned. It would be cold riding this morning.

Ben dressed quickly and went to stoke the fire in the wood stove. He threw in a small wedge of pine. As soon as the embers took hold of the fresh fuel and burst into flame, he closed the lid. He took the old weathered coffee pot off the shelf, filled it with cold water and a handful of coffee and placed it on the back of the stove. Soon the kitchen filled with the aroma of fresh perking coffee. With practiced hands, Ben finish frying three strips of bacon in a small cast iron skillet. Two fried eggs and toast put the finishing touches on his breakfast. He ate alone. His crew would be eating their breakfast in the cook shack.

After breakfast, Ben headed for the barn. His men were waiting for him. Sam was the first to speak. "Good mornin', boss. What's the orders for the day?"

"Sam, I'm glad you asked that question. Remember the blue roan filly? Well, I think it's time you two got to know each other better."

Sam groaned. "Is there any chance I could ride fence for the next month or two?"

"Sorry Sam. You're the best colt trainer I have. I can't let your talents be wasted mendin' fences." Ben grinned, delighting in teasing his friend.

The sound of an approaching truck drew their attention to the driveway. Ben recognized his friend's faded blue '92 Ford pickup and smiled. Gordon pulled in the driveway and parked his rig out of the way of the action. He unloaded a tall, lanky bay gelding. "Sorry I'm late, Ben. I had to help a late calvin' heifer this morning. Got a dandy bull calf out of her."

"That's okay. I'm runnin' a little late myself. We best get going though. It's going to be a long day in the saddle."

Ben and Sam saddled their horses. The three men mounted up and headed west towards the mountains. The early morning rays of the sun cast a golden pink glow off the snow fields and craggy rock walls of the Bitterroot Range. Shadows ran deep, giving a forbidding sense to the harshness of the terrain.

The three-year-old horses ranged on several acres of pasture land that extended back into the foothills of the mountains. If the horses were out in the open, it would not take long to bring them down to the ranch. However, if they were feeding in one of the many draws on their range, it would take several hours of riding to find and gather them.

The men rode in silence, each lost in their own thoughts, and Ben's were in turmoil. Earlier in the week he had received a disturbing letter from his sister in Chicago.

It had been a long time since he'd heard from her. Since her divorce, she had been struggling as a single parent. Ben was never quite sure how to comfort her. Now she was asking him if her teenage daughter could come and work for him during the summer. Ben had not seen his niece since she was a little girl. Now she was seventeen. Ben didn't know if he could live under the same roof with a female, a relative or not. He had been living a long time alone and was comfortable in his bachelor ways. Yet he did not feel he could turn her down either. His sister implied she was having trouble with her daughter. There were things that were said and unsaid in the letter that made him think it was serious. He figured he could handle a troubled boy, but a girl . . . ?

Ben finally broke the silence. "Boys, I have a problem, and I need some advice."

Gordon and Sam exchanged questioning looks. The bluntness of Ben's statement caught them both off guard. Gordon shifted his weight in the saddle and cleared his throat. He reached in his pocket for his chew before he answered. "Fire away, Ben. What's on your mind?"

"It's a woman problem." Ben felt the red creeping up into his face.

"Why, boss, I didn't even know you were datin'." Sam grinned.

Ben coughed and looked away. "It's nothin' like that. My sister from Chicago wrote and asked if her daughter could spend the summer with me, working for her keep. I just don't know what to tell her."

Gordon pulled his sweat-stained cowboy hat lower on his brow to shield his eyes from the brightness of the morning sun. "It seems to me, Ben, that havin' a feminine face around would add to the value of your spread."

Sam nodded his head in agreement. "It would be all right by me. I get tired of lookin' at the same old weather-beaten faces. A pretty gal sure would liven things up a bit."

"Maybe you fellas are right, but we're not runnin' a dude ranch. I don't want the men or myself to be saddled with the job of lookin' after some problem child." The humor had left Ben's face.

Sam squirmed in his saddle, easing his cold back muscles. "It seems to me she is a dude. The question is will she act like a dude?"

"Sam's right. Don't go passin' judgment on the girl. Just because she's from back East doesn't mean she can't hold her own." Gordon spit a long, brown stream of juice into the dirt.

Ben laughed heartily. "I believe you two could sell a drownin' man an anchor. I'll write to my sister tonight and tell her it's a deal . . . before I chicken out."

Gordon grinned. His ice blue eyes sparkled with good humor. "I'm glad you see it our way, Ben. What's this gal's name?"

"Elvira Parker."

Gordon and Sam looked at each other and grinned. Sam voiced what they were both thinking. "Does she come wearin' that black dress cut all the way down to her belt buckle?"

Ben grimaced. "She was born on Halloween. Her father thought it would be cute to name her after that famous Sixties Vamp, Elvira."

Sam coughed under his breath. "Some sense of humor. I'd have divorced him, too."

The men chuckled, hunching down in their coats against the cold. They topped out on a small hill. Ben reined in his horse. Gordon and Ben pulled up beside him. They looked down on an open grassy bench where a small group of horses grazed peacefully in the early morning sun. Suddenly, one of the horses threw up its head and stopped chewing, its ears swiveling to catch the wind. Ben grinned. It was the blue roan filly. He remembered well his first experience with her, the day they brought the colts in for weaning, two and a half years ago. Even at that age she had stood out among the terrified foals as they filled the air with their frantic neighing and the pounding of their tiny hooves. They had tried desperately to scramble up the walls of the weaning pen as the cowboys separated them from their mothers one-by-one and ran them into another corral. After several futile attempts to escape, most of them quit, but not the roan filly.

The hot, tiring work had taken most of the day, leaving men and horses drenched in sweat. With the sorting eventually done, the men had opened the heavy gate to the big pole corral and driven the mares back out to their winter range. It was a familiar routine to the older mares, but with this being the black mare's first foal, she resisted this forced separation from her blue roan filly. Again and again she had tried to return to the corrals, darting, dodging and wheeling in order to get by the men in her way. The cowboys blocked her every attempt, yelling and swinging their ropes, forcing her to rejoin the brood mare band. After being driven the two miles back to the fall pasture where she could no longer hear the calls of her foal, she gave up except for an occasional frantic whinny, and she made no more attempts to escape.

Ben recalled the scene in the weaning pens after the mares were taken away. For the first time in their lives the foals had lost the powerful sense of their mother's presence. The warmth and comfort of sweet mare's milk was lost forever. In fear and frustration, the more dominant foals kicked and bit the younger, more timid foals. Some tried to nurse their corral mates and received a swift kick for their efforts. When one of the cowboys came to the gate, they fled to the far side of the pen, nostrils flaring, and their eyes staring wildly. Then the gate opened, and an old bay gelding walked quietly into the enclosure. He was the baby sitter. Every fall he was put in with the weanlings to ease their fears and to teach them the ways of domestic life. The gelding looked briefly at the weanlings, then walked over to the big feeder full of hay and began to eat. The foals stood huddled together, watching the gelding.

The blue roan filly stomped a hoof in agitation. Then she took a few halting steps towards the old horse. He ignored her. Encouraged, she walked the rest of the way to the feeder and began to nibble tentatively at the hay. The other foals followed her example one-by-one until all of them were eating at the feeder. Occasionally, they would stop eating to pace around the pen and nicker plaintively for their mothers.

As the days passed, the foals settled into the ranch routine. Some had lost their voices from ceaseless whinnying, but as a whole, they quieted down and quit pacing the perimeters of the corral. The old gelding gave them great comfort, reducing their stress. They began to look forward to their hay and grain, and they lost some of their fear of the men who brought it.

The roan filly was the only one that went to the far side of the corral every time the gate opened. Ben remembered thinking how she was taking after her sire, the big rawboned blue roan Quarter Horse stallion he ran with his mare band. Like him, she was spooky and showed no signs of friendliness. She certainly did not have the gentle disposition of her dam. Ben prided himself in his breeding program. He had devoted thirty years studying pedigrees and foundation bloodlines, experimenting with different genetic crosses in order to develop outstanding performance horses, ones with that perfect combination of intelligence and physical conformation that made them exceptional ranch and arena horses. He had kept his rank old stud because the horse put good bone and endurance qualities into his offspring. By breeding him to quality, modern-type Quarter Horse mares, Ben hoped to weed out the stallion's bad disposition while maintaining the old horse's good traits. The mating of the roan stud to the black mare was to be the culmination of what he had learned from his years of trial and error. So far, this was beginning to look like another error.

Ben had given the foals two weeks to settle down, then on a clear fall morning he and the hired hands took down their ropes and headed for the corrals. Once again the foals were cut out, and one-by-one roped, haltered and tied to the stout posts of the round training pen. There they learned their strength was no match against the rope as they pulled back with all their might only to feel the halter press into the nerves at the back of their heads. Eventually, when their fear subsided, they figured out that to step forward eased the pressure and the pain. The blue filly was the last foal to be roped. She raced in a blind frenzy around the weaning pen.

"Let me have this one, boys." Ben shook out his loop. "She's kind of special. I'd like to get to know her better."

Ben started the filly running around him in a circle. At just the right moment, he threw his loop and caught her by both front feet. He braced himself as the filly hit the end of the rope and went down. Immediately one of the other cowboys grabbed her head. The filly kicked and struggled violently. Her teeth made clicking sounds as she snapped the air in her blind fury. The cowboy on her head was busy trying to keep his shirt on his back as he filly caught his sleeve between her teeth and ripped it off his arm.

The other hands watched in amusement as the filly took her toll on the cowboys. One of them piped up in good humor. "Ben, is this filly so special because her mama was a cougar?"

Ben worked the halter on to the filly's head. Sweat dripped from his brow, mingling with the sweat on the filly's neck. "She is a might touchy, isn't she?"

Ben, kneeling behind the filly, reached gingerly across her belly to loosen the rope around her ankles. He put a saddle blanket over her head to keep her quiet until Sam could get clear of her. When Ben removed the blanket, the filly leaped to her feet, striking with both front hooves at the enemy that had her by the head. As soon as her mad charge brought her near a post, Ben dallied the lead rope and jumped over the fence to get out of the way of her flying hooves.

Sam shook his head. "It'll be a miracle if she doesn't kill herself."

The filly fought the rope until her nose and mouth were bleeding from smashing into the fence. Finally, she quit struggling and pulled back on the rope, sulking.

Ben sighed. "Now isn't that the picture of perfect submission?"

Sam chuckled. "I can hardly wait until she's ready to ride. I bet she takes to bein' ridden like a duck takes to water." The rest of the hands smiled knowingly.

"Ben?" Gordon leaned over and touched Ben's arm. "Where'd you go?"

Ben shook the memories, clearing his head for the task at hand. "Sorry, I was just reminiscing."

At that moment, the blue roan filly gave one loud warning snort and bolted for the shelter of a nearby draw. The rest of the horses followed, trusting in her established dominant role as leader. Gordon's eyes closed to near slits as he scanned the trees for some sign of the direction the horses were headed. He turned to Sam and Ben. "I'm guessin' they'll head up he draw. We better ride up the ridge and come down ahead of them."

Ben reined his horse in the direction Gordon indicated. "Getting them out of the draw will be easy. It will be the run to the ranch that will make us sweat."

The three men rode the ridge until they spotted the horses hiding in the trees. Then they split up. Sam took the right side of the draw. Ben took the left and Gordon rode down the middle. When Gordon got close to the horses, he came at them whooping and hollering, riding hard. He didn't want to give them time to think of escape. Ben and Sam were riding fast, too, dodging trees and jumping windfalls. The cowboys had to hit the mouth of the draw at the same time the colts did so they could keep them bunched and lined out for the ranch.

The blue filly cleared the draw first and veered sharply to the right to make a break for the trees. Sam saw what she was doing, and swore under his breath. He put the spurs to his horse, causing it to leap forward into the path of the fleeing horse. For a frightening moment, it looked as if the filly was not going to stop, but at the last second she dug her hooves into the soft ground and swerved to miss Sam's horse. Sam pivoted his horse and shook out a loop. When the roan filly heard the hiss of the rope in the air, she ducked her head and shied back down the hill, losing her chance of escape. By this time Ben and Gordon had the other horses bunched and lined out for the ranch, but not for long.

In desperation, the blue filly wheeled away from Sam and charged through the middle of the colts, scattering them in every direction. Sam, Ben and Gordon raced their mounts to cut off the retreat of the young horses. By the time the herd was bunched again, both the men and the animals were slick with sweat. Once more, the men lined out the colts at a steady trot, heading in the direction of the Magruder ranch.

Finally, the gate of the old pole corral closed behind the last horse. The men leaned wearily against the rough poles, their bodies hot and itchy from dirt and sweat.

Gordon looked grim. "If I hadn't been afraid I'd break her neck, I would have roped and busted that blue bronc."

"I'm glad I wasn't carryin' a gun." Ben left it at that.

Sam stayed at the corral for a while after Ben and Gordon went to the ranch house. He watched the horses as they moved around the enclosure, and he studied their personalities. The roan filly took most of his attention. She moved light and quick; her feet barely seemed to touch the ground. When a buckskin gelding got in her way, she bit him viciously on the neck, leaving a bare patch of skin as he wheeled away to avoid her wrath. Every few minutes, the filly stopped to look at Sam with white-rimmed eyes that were filled with fear. She snorted defiantly in his direction.

Sam took his hat off and wiped his sleeve across his sweaty brow. "I have a feelin', blue horse, that between you and Miss Elvira Parker we're going to have a real interestin' summer."

ELVIRA

ELVIRA PARKER YAWNED and winced at the pounding ache that engulfed her head. She eyed the clock through heavy eyelids: seven a.m. Pulling the blankets over her head, she rolled over. Her waterbed rocked gently beneath her, bringing on a wave of nausea. If only she could stay in bed a little longer. She wondered, through the cloud of dull pain, if her mother had heard her throwing up in the bathroom most of the night. Well, what if she had? Ellie was sick of making excuses. Let her mother worry. What did she care?

"Ellie . . . time to get up. You'll be late for school."

She groaned. Her mother's loud voice shattered the last lingering hold she had on a chance to doze. "I'll be down in a minute, Mom."

Ellie threw back the covers, drew a deep breath to steady her sick stomach and crawled out of bed. As she entered the bathroom, she was hit in the face with the stench of last night's alcohol vomit. The smell caused her stomach to wretch and heave, but it was empty and nonproductive, leaving the bitter taste of bile on her tongue. Before getting into the shower, Ellie grabbed the Lysol spray from under the sink and filled the air with its perfumed aroma. She got into the shower, turned the water to steaming hot, and for twenty minutes tried to wash her misery down the drain. When she was done, Ellie wiped the steam from the mirror and took a close look. The face staring back at her was sallow. Dark circles detracted from her large green eyes, and her matted auburn hair stuck to her cheek. Ellie grimaced. She lifted a shaking hand to touch her high cheekbones. Her finger ran down her small angular nose and rested momentarily on the silver ring in her full bottom lip. "Talk about a bad hair day."

Ellie sighed. At seventeen she had everything, yet nothing. A senior at Chicago's Oak Park High, she still had no career plans, but her mother kept nagging at her to go to college. Ellie wasn't sure there was any point. She had no idea what she wanted to do with her life, nor did she care. The only thing she knew for sure was she would never marry. Angry words between her parents echoed in her memory. Her father's betrayal cut deep into her heart, leaving a festering wound that refused to heal.

"Your breakfast is ready." The impatient edge in her mother's voice told Ellie she'd better get downstairs.

"I'm coming." Parents were such a pain.

Ellie walked to the table and sat down. Her mom placed poached eggs and toast in front of her, along with a mug of hot chocolate. The sight of the food made Ellie's stomach heave. She swallowed hard and stirred the steaming mug in hopes of avoiding the food and her mother's questioning eyes. In a desperate move, she feigned interest. "How's work going?"

Her mother sighed. "It's going. That's about all I can say. There's not much hope of advancement for a cashier without an education."

Her mother's expression intensified. "Ellie, whatever you do, get a college education. Don't ever trust anybody to take care of you but yourself. You can't always count on having a husband."

Ellie watched her mother's face contort in anguish. After ten years, her mother's bitterness over her husband's leaving her still caused her pain. Ellie's throat tightened in anger, and she fought back the sting of her own tears. "Don't worry, Mom. I'm not dumb enough to fall into that trap."

The pain in her mother's eyes caused Ellie a momentary twinge of shame, but the power to hurt her mother also satisfied a certain unnamed need.

The shallow metallic clang of the mail slot cover banging shut startled them. Ellie got up from the table, eager to escape the conversation, and went to the living room. She picked up the small pile of letters and papers. Ellie frowned at the stack of bills. This was just what her mother needed to see. For a moment, she considered hiding them, but she knew that would only prolong the inevitable. As she thumbed through the bills, a smaller envelope fell to the floor. She picked it up and turned it over. Ellie didn't recognize the handwriting. The postmark indicated the point of origin as Hamilton, Montana.

Ellie frowned as she walked into the kitchen and handed the letter to her mother. "Mom, what's this?"

Her mother hesitated for a moment before she answered. "It's a letter from your uncle in Montana."

"My uncle? I forgot I even had one. Why would he be writing to you now? It's not Christmas."

With trembling fingers, Ellie's mother tore open the envelope. She quickly scanned over the lines. Avoiding Ellie's eyes, she explained. "A few weeks ago I wrote to your Uncle Ben asking him if you could spend the summer with him on his ranch. He says yes. Isn't that great, honey?"

Ellie stared at her mother in disbelief. "OMG, you did what?"

"Well, you just seem so unhappy lately. You're not sleeping or eating enough. I thought the change might do you some good."

"Did it ever occur to you that I might not want a change? I've got plans for the summer, and going to BFE isn't included."

Anger flashed in her mother's eyes. "Don't be vulgar. Plans? You've got plans? Partying and hanging out at the mall don't lead to a very productive life."

Ellie shook her head. "Is that all you care about . . . money? I'm sorry, but I happen to think there're more important things in life." She turned her back on her mother and started to leave.

Her mom watched her retreating daughter and launched her last desperate shot. "What are you afraid of Ellie?" She paused, then added, "It's probably just as well. You couldn't survive a summer away from your mall rat friends."

Ellie hesitated for a second before heading for the door. "Whatevs." She knew her mother's psychological ploys. She wasn't going to take the bait this time. Ellie grabbed her school bag and slammed the door on her way out.

The big orange school bus pulled away from the curb as Ellie ran down the sidewalk. "Hey, wait for me!" She ran a few steps, but her head spun, and her stomach heaved, so she stopped. Ellie yelled at the retreating bus. "What do I friggin' care? I didn't wanna go to school anyway."

Pulling her cell phone out of her purse, she punched in a number, then another and another. Finally, there was a response. "Hello. Allisha, I knew I could count on you. I missed the bus. Might as well make the most of it. Let's skip and go to the mall. Better yet, let's get a six pack and go to the park. Pick me up at the Zip Trip on Eighth and Elm. okay. See you in a bit."

Ellie slipped her smartphone into her back jean pocket and headed down the sidewalk. By the time she reached the Zip Trip, her head was pounding so hard she could barely see. She pushed the door open and headed for the bathroom. When she came out, she grabbed a package of aspirin and headed to the counter. She saw Allisha drive up in her new black Mustang, an early graduation present. Ellie smiled sadly to herself. If Allisha kept skipping school, she wouldn't be graduating. She watched as Allisha got out of the car and headed for the store.

Again, Ellie smiled to herself. She and Allisha were quite the odd couple. Ellie knew she would never have the guts to get her body tattooed the way Allisha had done, nor could she bring herself to dye her hair purple and spike it like her friend's. Her mother would've pitched a fit. Putting their differences aside, Allisha was a true friend whom she could count on for understanding and good times.

As her friend came through the door, Ellie waved. "Over here, Allisha."

Allisha smiled and joined Ellie. "Damn, you look awful. You sure you want to do this?"

"No, but I couldn't think of a good excuse to stay home. If my mom finds out about this, I'll be grounded for life."

"You worry too much. I'll grab us a couple of six packs, and we're out of here."

Ellie watched as Allisha grabbed two six packs from the cooler and went to the checkout. Allisha flashed her fake ID with a coolness born of success. The cashier looked at the ID and then at Allisha. She flashed him a charming smile. He seemed to shrug as he took her money, but said nothing. Soon the two girls were out the door and in the Mustang.

Ellie ran her hand lovingly over the black leather seat. "Wow. I still can't believe your parents got you this car."

"Yah, I know. I think they're feeling guilty for being gone so much. A little guilt goes a long way." Allisha shifted gears and whipped expertly through traffic.

Buck and the Blue Roan

Six hours later, Allisha dropped Ellie off in front of her house. She swung out of the car and stood up on weak legs. Ellie steadied herself before closing the car door. "Thanks, Allisha. See you tomorrow."

Allisha looked at Ellie and flashed a crooked grin. "By the looks of you, I'm guessing probably not. Good luck making it past the guard." With that, she floored the accelerator, leaving behind a cloud of smoking rubber.

Ellie walked up the sidewalk, trying not to teeter or stumble. She grabbed the iron railing and pulled herself up the steps. Reaching the top, she stopped to quiet her stomach and gather her courage. Finally, she grabbed the doorknob and slowly turned it until she felt the latch release. Ellie held her breath as she pushed the door open and entered the hallway.

"Elvira, where have you been?"

The hurt and anger in her mother's voice made Ellie suddenly very sober. Ellie tried to sound convincing. "I've been at school. Why?"

Ellie's mother moved very close to her and looked her in the eyes. Ellie could see that she had been crying. "You're lying!"

The words struck Ellie with the force of a physical blow. "Seriously, Mom? What about all your lies about Dad? Hm? I'm going to my room. Get out of my way."

Ellie's mom raised her hand to stop her. "Don't! I'm sick of it. The school called today wondering where you were. I had to go in and meet with the principle. Bottom line . . . you're expelled for the rest of the year. Happy graduation."

Ellie pushed past her mother. "I don't friggin' care!"

The next day, Ellie left the house before her mom woke up. She wandered for blocks, not caring where her feet took her. An hour later she found herself outside of the Zip Trip. She pulled the glass door open and walked in. The cashier looked up briefly, then returned to the magazine he was reading.

Ellie was feeling the effects of her long walk. Her stomach ached, and her mouth tasted disgusting. She eyed the beer case and then looked at the cashier. He was lost in his magazine. Ellie had left the house without her purse. It was a long walk back home, and she knew Allisha would ignore her texts this early in the morning. Ellie wandered up and down the aisles trying to work up her courage. She'd watched Allisha shoplift several times and get away with it. It didn't look that difficult. Ellie decided against trying to grab a bottle of beer. She knew from the talk around school the consequences of a MIP. Finally, Ellie picked her target: a can of energy drink. She looked over her shoulder to see if anyone was watching. Another shopper had his back to her. Ellie quickly slipped the slender can up her coat sleeve and casually walked out the door.

From seemingly out of nowhere, a strong hand grabbed her wrist. "Going somewhere, miss?"

Ellie tried to pull away. "Let me go. I have to get home."

The security guard tightened his grip. "Not a chance. I've been watching you. What do you have up your sleeve?"

Ellie stood silently as the man reached up her coat sleeve and pulled out the colorful energy drink. "What do we have here? You can come back inside and wait for the cops. The boss is tired of little punks like you lifting his merchandise. He wants to send a message. It looks like you drew the short straw, sweetheart."

The security guard took Ellie to a back room and forced her to sit down. Twenty minutes later, she was cuffed and put in the back seat of a patrol car, taken to jail and booked into juvenile detention. As the cell door closed behind her, Ellie stared in despair at the bare walls surrounding her. Now what? Her mother had been cold and distant on the phone. She wasn't coming to pick her up. Ellie spent a sleepless night wondering what the morning would bring.

The next morning, Ellie was escorted into a courtroom. She saw several parents seated with teens of various ages. Her mother sat near the back of the room.

"Good morning, Elvira. Her mother's voice was flat, and Ellie could see she'd been crying.

"Mom, I . . ."

Her mother raised her hand. "I don't want to hear it."

Without fanfare, the judge entered the courtroom. Everyone stood briefly, then sat back down. Ellie's case was low on the docket. She chewed her nails to the quick until they bled. She fidgeted until her mother's glare made her stop. Finally, the judge called her name. She and her mother went forward.

The judge was an attractive woman with white hair and blue eyes. When she addressed Ellie, she didn't smile. "Miss Parker, I have been reviewing your records. Your truancy numbers are problematic. And now you are being charged with petty theft from a retail establishment. Are you aware of the seriousness of this situation?"

Ellie stared at the floor. She could hardly speak. When she did, it was barely audible. "Yes, your honor."

The judge continued. "I have several options. Mrs. Parker, do you wish to make any comments?"

Ellie's mother looked at her daughter and sighed. "Your honor, I am at a complete loss. I can't seem to get through to my daughter anymore. I do have a brother in Montana who said he'd take her for the summer."

The judge nodded thoughtfully. "I recommend a diversion program for your daughter. Miss Parker, I sentence you to spend six months under the guardianship of your uncle. You will also have a mandated technology fast: no cell phone and no computer access. Do you understand?"

The judge's last statement was a slap in the face. Ellie wanted to scream in protest, but she held her tongue. "Yes, your honor."

"I'm releasing you to your parent. I suggest you make some life changes. I never want to see you in my court again."

"Yes, your honor." Ellie had never felt so humiliated. She kept her head down as she and her mother left the courtroom. She hated her life; she hated her mother, and more than anything, she hated the thought of going to Montana.

After a phone call, and with her brother's help, her mother purchased one e-ticket to Missoula, Montana. Ellie's uncle and his ranch loomed frighteningly in her future. At the end of the week, she said goodbye to her mother at O'Hare International Airport and boarded a jet bound for Montana.

She found her seat over the wing near the window and settled in, hoping she looked old enough to be served alcohol, because right now she needed a drink more than any time she could remember. Ellie cringed at the sound of the powerful jet engines as they revved for take-off, knowing there was no turning back.

The plane taxied down the runway and began to pick up speed. She closed her eyes and concentrated on the sensation of speed and power. The jet lifted off the ground and banked gently as it headed west. Ellie opened her eyes, took a small mirror from her purse and checked her makeup. Yes, the dark plum lipstick and sable eyeshadow made her look older than her seventeen years. She turned in her seat and motioned to the flight attendant. "Miss, could I please have a Screwdriver?"

♦♦♦

Ben Magruder woke with a sense of anxiety. His niece was arriving at Missoula Airport today, and he was not at all sure he was ready to receive her into his home. At times like this, he missed the feminine touch of his wife. He had given away most of her things that decorated their home: the oak spinning wheel that used to be in the corner by the fire, the hand-stitched quilts from the couches and the piano. It wasn't that he didn't value the memory of his wife; it was just the presence of her things had mocked the emptiness she'd left behind.

Now he wished he hadn't been so hasty. The rooms of the log ranch house stood bare, making the emptiness seem even bigger. He could only hope that his Spartan surroundings wouldn't discourage his new guest from making herself feel at home.

Ben ate a leisurely breakfast. His niece's plane didn't arrive until late afternoon. After he cleaned up the dishes and searched the house for stray items of dirty laundry, he headed for the corrals. He needed something to take his mind off his anxiety over meeting Elvira.

Dust rising out of the corrals indicated that Sam was already at work. Ben walked over and looked between the rails. Sure enough, Sam had an unruly colt on the end of a training halter. He was in the process of desensitizing the horse with an old slicker. The sorrel gelding snorted, rolled his eyes and trembled in fear. His coat glistened with sweat. Every time Sam shook the slicker, the youngster reared back on the rope, trying to pull away. Sam kept coming closer, all the time talking to the colt in a slow, soothing voice. When Sam was close enough, he put his hand on the colt's shoulder. The colt jumped as if touched with a red-hot iron. Sam just kept talking and touching until the horse quit trying to pull away from him. Then Sam began rubbing him and slapping him with the slicker. The colt soon realized he wasn't being hurt, so he quit spooking and accepted the strange behavior. Sam, satisfied with the youngster's response, gave him a final pat on the neck and turned him loose.

As Sam turned to catch another colt, he spotted Ben standing by the fence. "Good mornin', boss. Say, you're lookin' mighty fine."

Ben felt the heat rising in his face. "I know it's a shock to see me in a clean pair of jeans, but I have important business to tend to today."

Sam tipped his hat back off his head and mopped the sweat from his brow with a faded blue bandanna. "That's right. Today's the day the gal from back east comes."

"Yup. And I don't mind tellin' you the prospect makes me as skittish as a green broke bronc on a cold mornin'." In spite of Ben's grin, there was a real note of seriousness in his voice. He'd been forewarned by his sister that this was not going to be an easy visit.

Sam smiled and gave Ben an understanding wink. "She'll do fine, boss. You'll see."

"I hope you're right." Ben looked doubtful. "Changin' the subject, I got a call from Ed Eagle Plume up in the Flathead Valley. He asked me to keep my eyes open for a good heelin' horse. Seems they lost one earlier this spring. Do you think any of this bunch would do?"

"There's a couple of nice geldings comin' along. The blue roan filly's built for it, but I don't think she'll have the disposition."

"I was hopin' giving her an extra year might help settle her down. Have you started her yet?"

"No, I'm savin' the best for last." Sam grinned.

"I invited Ed and his son over to see them, so I hope she'll be ready. I figure even though they probably want a gelding, I might be able to impress them with her genetic potential." Ben checked his watch for the tenth time that morning. "It looks like it's time for me to go. I have some things to get done in Missoula before the plane gets in. Take it easy, Sam."

"I will, boss. The same to you." Sam picked up his rope. As the dust from Ben's pickup was rising over the driveway, Sam was throwing his loop on another horse.

♦♦♦

The "buckle your seatbelt" sign flashed on as Ellie felt the plane bank for its final approach to the Missoula airport. Looking out the window, she saw a flat plain surrounded by mountains that still had snow on them. At one end of the valley, a large factory of some sort belched a plume of white smoke high into the air.

She watched as the ground came up to meet the jet, and braced herself for the landing. As the plane taxied to the terminal, Ellie's mind swirled with doubts. What was she doing here? If she didn't like it or couldn't take it, she was in trouble, but she knew she couldn't admit defeat. Her mother's challenge echoed in her mind, reminding her that there was no going back. Another troubling thought struck her. What if nobody came to meet her? Ellie wasn't sure she could recognize her uncle. She vaguely remembered his face in the wedding photographs of her mother, but they were taken a long time ago.

Once the plane came to a stop and the door opened, popping another stick of gum into her mouth, she gathered a small overnight bag from the overhead bin and worked her way down the aisle.

"Goodbye. Hope you had a pleasant flight." The flight attendants bade their passengers farewell.

Ellie, startled out of her thoughts, hoped she was walking steadier than she felt. "Oh, . . . goodbye. Thank you."

She walked up the ramp to the concourse, vaguely amused by the sharp contrast between this airport and the one she'd just left a few short hours ago. O'Hare International reminded her of an anthill, everyone rushing around trying to find the right tunnel to go down. Here people acted so casual. There were no agitated passengers pushing or shoving as if their lives depended on getting off their plane. Ellie smiled to herself as she walked into the terminal that didn't seem much larger than a convenience store back home.

"Elvira, is that you?"

Ellie looked up at the sound of the masculine voice. She saw an elderly man smiling at her. Something in his face reminded her of her mother. "Uncle Ben?"

"That's me, gal." Ben Magruder took Ellie's small hand and shook it enthusiastically. The power of his grasp amazed her. She couldn't remember the last time she'd shaken hands with anyone. It was a weird feeling.

An awkward silence followed as Ellie searched for something to say to this total stranger. Finally, she came up with what she thought was a lame remark. "Thanks for coming to get me."

"Elvira, I'm mighty pleased to have you come. I miss havin' family near." Ben turned his hat around in his big hands.

Ellie grimaced. "I hate that name. Dad named me after some '60's vamp, probably when he was high, so please call me Ellie. That's what my friends call me."

Ben smiled awkwardly. "Okay, Ellie it is. Now, we'd better get your luggage and head for the ranch.

After a short wait at the baggage conveyor, Ellie claimed her two green brocade suitcases. "That's everything. We can go."

Ben started chuckling. "I can't figure you women out. I brought the pickup because I thought sure you'd bring half of Chicago with you, and you turn up with what looks like luggage for a two-week stay."

Ellie smiled in spite of herself. "You should see the mess I left behind. I couldn't make up my mind what to bring. I can hardly wait to go shopping. Is there a mall near where you live?"

Ben gulped. "Uh . . . well. We can see about that."

Ellie shrugged her shoulders and climbed into Ben's sapphire blue Ford pickup. It was a strange sensation sitting so high up in a vehicle. She liked being able to see all around her, and it gave her a strange sense of power. This new feeling lasted for the hour and a half drive from the airport to the Magruder ranch.

Ben and Ellie spent most of the trip in silence. Ben asked her an occasional question about her mother, but mostly he left her alone to enjoy the mountains and the contrasting green summer colors of the fruitful valley. On the east side of the Bitterroot River valley, low rolling hills flowed back to green forested mountains, but it was the mountains on the west side of the valley that took her breath away. They were high and jagged with chiseled cliffs and crags. The snow-covered summits stood out boldly against the evening sky. Deep, narrow canyons with steep walls made mysterious passages back into the mountains, beckoning to be explored.

The sun was low in the west by the time they drove into Hamilton. Ben indicated a small café. "How about a bite to eat?"

Ellie needed something to get rid of the stale taste of vodka in her mouth. "Sounds good to me. I'm starving."

Ben pulled into the parking lot. "I'm glad we're eatin' here. I wasn't sure what I was going to fix for us to eat tonight."

Ellie looked surprised. "You do the cooking?"

"Yup, ever since my wife died."

"Maybe I can help you sometimes. Do you have a microwave?"

Ben shook his head. "I never saw much need for one. I'm pretty much a fried steak and potatoes man."

Ellie decided to let the microwave issue drop. She and Ben enjoyed a quiet country meal of fried chicken, mashed potatoes and milk gravy. Again, Ellie was struck by the differences between this small café and the fancy restaurants of Chicago. She was sorry to leave the cozy atmosphere of the café but was tired enough to take Ben's advice about heading home.

It was almost dark when Ben turned the truck onto the gravel road that led to the Magruder ranch. Ellie strained her eyes, trying to see everything in the near dark. With no stoplights or street signs to mark their progress, she felt like they'd been driving for an eternity. Finally, Ben pulled into a driveway surrounded by several buildings. Lights were shining in two of them.

Ben stopped the pickup in front of a large house that sat back away from the rest of the buildings. Its rustic log walls looked like a fortress in the fading light. He turned off the truck engine. "Well, here we are."

"Is this it?"

"Come mornin' I'll give you a grand tour of the ranch. It's much bigger in the daylight. Right now we have to get your stuff unloaded and into the house.

Ben opened the door and got out of the pickup. Ellie grabbed her overnight case and followed him up the stairs and onto the porch of the log ranch house. Surprised at how cold and crisp the evening air was, she welcomed the warmth of the house as she stepped into the living room. Suddenly, Ellie felt as if she'd stepped back in time and had entered the home of a wealthy rancher baron. The living room was half the size of a gym with a fire burning cheerfully in a large stone fireplace at one end of the room. A rifle rested in an impressive rack of elk horns over the fireplace. Navajo throw rugs complemented the pine floor. Several western paintings hung on the walls. The furniture looked solid and rugged. Ellie wasn't sure she liked it.

"Uncle Ben, it's . . . there's so much wood!" Ellie walked around the room, trying to take it all in at once.

"It's plain and simple, but it's home for me." Ben said.

"Here, let me show you to your room." He led Ellie down a short hallway and into a room on the right.

She walked over to the bed and touched the homemade quilt tentatively. "I've read about these in books. This is the first one I've ever seen. It's sick."

Ben's eyes narrowed at the word. "It was made by a lovely woman. My wife made it the winter before she passed away. It's the only thing of hers I've kept."

Ellie looked up at this gentle man she barely knew. Her heart momentarily melted, making her uncharacteristically soft. "Wow . . . cool . . . I mean . . ."

Ben cleared his throat. "I'll leave you alone to get settled for the night. I think I'm going to turn in myself. Tomorrow will be a busy day." He turned to leave.

"Um . . . goodnight, I guess."

Ellie closed the door behind him and turned to inspect the room that was to be her home for the next six months. The room was small but not confining. The log walls were decorated with more western art. A simple pine chest of drawers stood against one wall, a white cotton dust cover with hand embroidery covering it. Ellie fingered the delicate stitches, wondering about the woman who'd made them. She'd never seen anything like it. The finest part of the room was the big brass double bed with its hand-stitched quilt. Ellie walked to it and sat down, gently testing the mattress. The light from the lamp on the bedside stand glistened on the polished brass. Everything about the room spoke of love and tender care, something intangible that left Ellie suddenly feeling even more depressed than she usually did.

She unpacked her suitcases, hung up her clothes and placed a few bottles of perfume and a picture of her parents on the pine dresser. For a moment, she focused on her father, wondering where he was and why he'd left. She'd not gotten over her feeling of bitterness, and the guilt and pain were never far away. "Dad, what did I do to make you hate me so much?"

Tired and emotionally spent, Ellie decided to call it a day. She took her overnight bag into the bathroom across the hall. Several miniature airline vodka bottles rattled against each other as she reached for her toothbrush. Luckily, the college student next to her on the plane had been willing to part with his. Ellie counted the bottles, only four, enough for two days if she could control herself. Panic seized her, but she fought it off. She would search the house for a liquor cabinet first chance she got.

She returned to her room and crawled gratefully under the heavy covers. Feeling like a little girl again, all snug and safe in the depths of the big brass bed, Ellie rolled over and looked out the bedroom window. The stars were framed by the boughs of a tall pine tree outside. Never had she seen a night so black nor the stars so clear and bright. Never had she felt so small. She hugged her pillow and sobbed. Alisha, Chicago, her cell phone; Ellie's sense of loss overwhelmed her. Between sobs, she whispered, "Star light, star bright, first star I see tonight. Wish I may, wish I might, have the wish I wish tonight."

My Friends Call Me Ellie

BUCK PACED THE FLOOR, giving his worn, red beanbag a hard kick as he walked by. It wasn't just the loss of Chester that spurred his restless walking. The emotions festering in his heart went much deeper. Anger and hurt made him miserable. He was mad at his grandfather and frustrated because he was not able to break through the wall his grandfather had encased himself in. His earliest memories of his grandfather were feelings more than images; feelings of fear, hurt and disappointment. His grandfather lived to work, and what time he'd been home was spent caring for Rusty. After his son and daughter-in-law had been killed by a drunk driver, Ed Eagle Plume had pulled away from everyone. The only time he gave to Buck was the time shared with horses, and now they didn't even have much of that. Now, when Buck needed his grandfather more than ever, he seemed to be far away, out of reach.

A loud knock on the bedroom door jarred Buck out of his gloomy reflections. "Yah?"

"It's me. May I come in?"

"I guess so." Buck went to the door and opened it for his grandfather.

Ed Eagle Plume entered the room, avoiding Buck's eyes as he crossed the floor and sat down in an old wooden rocker near the window. Buck plopped down on his bed, hands behind his head, staring at the ceiling.

Buck's grandfather cleared his throat. "I've always tried to be straight with you, so I'll get right to the point. It's pretty plain that somethin' big is botherin' you. If you feel like talkin', I'm here to listen. If not, I'll be on my way."

Buck was silent for a long time. When he finally spoke, his words came slow. He struggled to paint a picture of the turmoil in his heart, afraid to say the words he really wanted to say. "I don't think I believe in your dreams anymore. It doesn't seem to matter. Without Chester, I'm dead meat. I can kiss a pro-rodeo career goodbye."

He wanted to shock his grandfather, to hurt him, to get him to react, anything to put a crack in the wall. He wasn't prepared for his grandfather's reply.

"Buck, you're not the only one who's hurting. If you'd quit indulging your self-pity, you'd see that. And, it's not *my* dream; it's *our* dream. It only becomes my dream if you walk away from it."

Buck knew better, but like the moth dancing its death on a flame, he couldn't stop. "You should know. You're an expert on walking away. After Mom and Dad were killed, when I needed you most, you shut me out."

Silence. Buck strained his ears, hoping for some sound to ease the weight of his words in the air, but he couldn't hear anything. He longed for Rusty to come bursting through the door like he always did. His grandfather never seemed to be able to stay angry when Rusty was around, but Rusty wasn't coming. Buck needed to clear his throat, but he was afraid the sound might break loose his grandfather's emotions, and he would then feel the full force of the big man's wrath. He hoped for it, yet he feared it. He remembered his grandfather's anger from the times he saw him confront his mother when she was drunk. It scared him so bad, he'd hidden under his bed.

However, Ed didn't respond but stood and headed toward the door. He stopped on his way out of the bedroom, his voice uncharacteristically cold. "By the way, I got an invitation from Ben Magruder to have a look at his horses. He has several good geldings. I thought I'd drive down Saturday and take a look at them. It's your call if you want to come along."

Buck threw his pillow at the closing door as his grandfather walked out of the room. He swore, but not loud enough for his grandfather to hear. "Someday, Grandfather, you're going to have to give me an answer. You won't always be able to hide behind horses. Some day.

♦♦♦

It was nine o'clock in the morning, and Ben had been up since six. No sounds were coming from Ellie's room. He sighed. The ranch had been in full swing for two hours, and she was still in bed. If this was her normal pattern of living, she was in for a shock. No ranch hand of Ben Magruder's was going to lie around in bed all morning, girl or not.

He went to the stove and poured another cup of coffee. The mornings were still cold. The warmth of the hot liquid going down his throat felt good.

"I hope I'm not too late for breakfast."

Ben was in the middle of swallowing his coffee. Startled by Ellie's voice, he choked and sputtered. Ellie stood in the doorway of the kitchen. She was wrapped in a soft emerald robe. Her thick auburn hair cascaded down around her shoulders. Ben could only stand and stare at her, disconcerted by the shining ring through her lip.

"Uncle Ben, are you all right?"

"Yah, you just took me by surprise." Ben picked up the morning paper to hide his embarrassment.

Ellie searched the cupboards until she found the coffee mugs. She poured herself some coffee and went to the table to sit down.

Ben cleared his throat. "You used to sleepin' in?"

"Well, I guess mom babies me a bit during summer vacation. She always lets me sleep in. It makes up for all those early mornings getting to the school bus.

Ben shook his head. "You're missin' out on the best part of the day. It gets a person's blood going to get up when the dew's still on the grass and the mornin's fresh and new."

"Yeah, I'd like to do that one of these days." Ellie rolled her eyes.

Ben shot back at her. "Good. You can start tomorrow. I like to have breakfast at six-thirty. I'll leave the cookin' and shoppin' up to you. I can trust you with the grocery money, can't I?"

Ellie frowned and sighed dramatically. "Well, I guess I know my place around here. What else am I expected to do?"

Ben felt a little sorry for Ellie, but her tone irritated him. She looked small, tired and fragile sitting there, so he gave her the benefit of the doubt. He was almost afraid to tell her what he did expect from her, but he wouldn't baby his niece. He would treat her just like everyone else working for him. He would give her a chance to prove herself. For now, he would start by answering her questions. "I'd like you to take over the house: cook, clean and be hostess when we have company. Then if you feel like you have enough spare time, we can put in the garden."

Ben noticed the dark cloud of emotion gathering on Ellie's face. Her green eyes shone with a strange blackness. He wondered if she was going to blow up. Well, if she was, his next remark ought to make her cut loose. "You'll get your first chance to play hostess this Saturday. I've invited a friend of mine and his son over for the day. They're comin' to look at the horses. I'd like to have a big noon meal for them."

Ellie didn't say anything for a long time.

"Ellie, you can do that, can't you?"

"I'll try my best, Uncle Ben," she conceded.

"Well, that's all I can ask from anybody." Ben smiled warmly.

Ellie sighed and appeared to relax. "Uncle Ben, I'd like to see the ranch if that's cool."

"Little lady, for you we have the grand tour." Ben took Ellie's small soft hands into his big rough ones and gave them a gentle squeeze.

♦♦♦

Buck loved the early morning hours when the robins were singing. He was glad to see them after the long hard winter. This morning their song seemed to carry a promise of something good. Buck was glad his grandfather had asked him to go along on the trip to the Magruder ranch. The tension between them made each day a misery. Buck was ready for some excitement, a new challenge, anything to get him going again and to take his grandfather's mind off the strain between them. Maybe it was best just to pretend everything was okay and get on with his life. He smiled grimly at the irony of the situation. He lived in the biggest, most free land a man could be in, yet he felt as cooped up as if he were in prison. A man was only free when he was at peace with himself, but for now, peace eluded him.

"Well, Buck, are you ready to go?" Ed had driven down to the barn to pick up Buck on his way out of the driveway.

"Yup, chores are all done." Buck climbed up into the truck. "You takin' the horse trailer along just for the fun of it?" Buck enjoyed teasing his grandfather about his weakness for fine horses. It was a real struggle for Ed to resist buying a good horse when he saw one.

"You never know. We might find a top ropin' prospect. No sense makin' two trips." Ed glanced at Buck, and the tightness in his jaw seemed to relax a little.

The warmth of the early morning sun shining through the truck window was contrasted pleasantly with the deep snow still covering the Mission Mountains. Ed and Buck drove Highway 93 in silence, enjoying the panoramic view of the mountains, but unsure of each other. After they had passed through Missoula, heading south, they entered the Bitterroot Valley. A sense of anticipation charged the air. Ed broke the silence. "I can't get over how this country keeps changin'. I'm afraid civilization is takin' over the valley."

"Well, Grandfather, I don't think you need to worry until Sula gets more than one paved street."

Ed chuckled. "I guess you're right. I just hope the old-time ranchers can hang on to what they have."

Buck hoped so, too. Just last fall their neighbors had to sell their ranch to keep them from losing it to the bank. Either way, they lost. The troubled economy made it hard on the ranchers and their families. He loved ranching, but he honestly didn't know if there was any future in it. Bad cattle prices and drug abuse drove many of the young kids off the reservation to the big cities, leaving many of the old spreads to be reclaimed by the bank and the harsh conditions of Montana's climate.

Ed changed the subject. "You remember the black filly Ben paid such a big price for about ten years ago?"

"Sure. He had pretty high hopes for her didn't he?"

"He's bettin' the ranch on her. Her first foal is in this bunch of young horses they're breakin'—a blue roan filly."

"Now, Grandfather, don't go settin' your sights on a mare. You know they're temperamental and inconsistent. They just don't make a reliable rope horse."

"Buck, don't get narrow-minded on me. There've been a lot of good ropers mounted on mares. Mares can have more drive, and they can pass on their traits to their foals. Why, a good mare is worth her weight in gold."

"Okay, Grandfather, you win. I'll try to keep an open mind, but I can't see saddlin' myself with a temperamental four-legged female."

♦♦♦

Ellie tried to ignore the butterflies in her stomach. She wished now she'd paid more attention to the art of cooking when she'd been in Home Ec. She also needed a drink desperately. She'd had her last airline bottle before breakfast, and she still hadn't had a chance to find out if Ben had a liquor cabinet.

Uncle Ben hadn't given her much time to prepare herself for her new duties. She'd been too embarrassed to go to the cook and ask for help. Instead, she gathered up Ben's meager collection of cookbooks and wore herself out reading recipes. She'd been so worried about the weekend she couldn't even enjoy Ben's "grand tour" of the ranch. In fact, she could remember very little about it except that it was all so big. Now, it was Saturday, and Ellie felt as if she'd forgotten something. Carefully she ran over the details of the meal in her mind. She'd finally decided on fried chicken. That sounded like a safe thing to tackle. A box cake mix solved the dessert problem.

Uncle Ben's cupboards contained the strangest assortment of plates, cups and saucers Ellie'd ever seen. There were old mugs with broken handles. None of the saucers matched the other cups. There were blue, salmon and green Melmac plates that had seen better days. She decided to use the China plates she found in the Oak hutch in the corner of the dining room. They were a little elaborate for a Saturday lunch, but she felt they were more appropriate than the odds and ends in the kitchen.

The honking of a truck horn brought her attention to the kitchen window. Ellie looked out and saw a blue and white pickup with a matching horse trailer pulling into the driveway. Panic seized her. Uncle Ben said he wanted lunch served by noon because he wanted to be in the house to hear his favorite news broadcaster. It was a daily ritual with him. Ellie looked at the clock. She didn't have much time. All Uncle Ben had in his freezer was whole fryers. She'd never dealt with a whole chicken before. She knew it had to be cut up before she could cook it, but she didn't know it was supposed to be thawed first. She just wasn't sure how or where to start. Ellie picked up a formidable looking butcher knife in one hand and daintily took the chicken carcass in the other. Her hands were trembling. Now, where to make the first cut
. . .?

Ben waved to the approaching pickup. When they pulled up and got out, Buck and his grandfather were greeted with a broad grin and Ben's powerful handshake. "I sure am glad you fellas could make it down today. I've got a lot of fine horses to show you."

Ed Eagle Plume grinned. He was well aware of Ben's enthusiasm for good horses. He knew they would not only be shown the three-year-olds but every other horse on the ranch as well. "That's what we came down for Ben, to see these fine horses you're always braggin' about."

Ben took the teasing good-naturedly. "It's not a brag. It's fact, just pure fact."

"Well, let's get started then."

"Good, we'll take my truck and drive out to the north pasture to see the new crop of colts."

The three men got in Ben's pickup and headed out over the bumpy pasture road. Several wire gates later, the truck topped a small hill and came to a stop. Buck let out a soft whistle.

"It's a pretty sight isn't it?" Ben's face shone with pride.

Buck nodded his head. "No matter how many times I see it, the sight of mares and foals out on pasture always gives me a thrill."

The men got out of the truck and walked among the gentle band of mares. The foals were curious but kept a safe distance between themselves and the strange two-legged creatures walking among them.

Ed pointed out a nice red roan colt. "Look at the muscling in that little fella's hindquarters."

Buck added his evaluation. "He looks like he'll have more than his share of speed when he grows up."

Several other colts caught the eye of Buck and his grandfather. Ben glowed under the praise. Finally, Ed shook his head in amazement. "Well, Ben, I have to admit it looks like all the talk I heard is fact."

Ben grinned. "I'm savin' the beast for last. Right now we better head back, or we'll miss out on lunch. Can't keep the cook waitin'."

Ed looked surprised. "What happened Ben?" Did you get so tired of your own cookin' you had to hire a new housekeeper?"

Ben had an impish sparkle in his eyes. "Yes, in a way, I did."

No more was said about the new cook. Buck's mind was so occupied with evaluating the horses he completely missed the conversation between Ben and his grandfather. There was no question about the quality of Ben's horses, but most of them were too young to be of any use to him. What he needed was a five or six-year-old gelding that had a lot of miles on him with cow experience. He didn't have the time to waste on the training of a young horse.

The sound of the approaching pickup filtered into Ellie's mind, causing her to look up at the clock. It was five minutes to twelve. She groaned, feeling desperately close to tears. The chicken had almost won the fight with the butcher knife. The mashed potatoes were full of tiny uncooked chunks. The gravy was . . . well, she'd never seen anything quite like it before. Ellie, herself, was showing signs of the culinary battle she'd been waging. Her apron was stained with grease and blood, not all of it the chicken's blood. There was flour on her face where she'd brushed back strands of loose hair. She was hot, tired and not at all ready to face the three men she heard enter the house.

Ben led his guests into the spacious living room. "You fellas make yourselves at home while I go see how our lunch is comin'. The bathroom's down the hall and to the left."

Buck and his grandfather went to clean up while Ben headed into the kitchen. He stopped short, overwhelmed by the chaos. In the middle of it stood the most pathetic looking female he'd seen in a long time. He forced cheerfulness into his voice. "Somethin' sure smells good around here."

"Oh, Uncle Ben!" Ellie wailed.

"Now gal, don't you worry. You just go get cleaned up, and I'll put things out on the table for you."

"Thanks, Uncle Ben." She gave her uncle a crushing hug and hurried from the room.

Ellie soon returned with the dirty apron gone. Her clean face and her combed hair gave her a look of renewed confidence.

Ben gave her a reassuring smile, then called his guests to the table. Buck and his grandfather came into the dining room and stood by the chairs Ben indicated.

"Fellas, I'd like you to meet my niece, Elvira Parker. She came out here from Chicago to spend the summer."

Ellie felt the heat rising in her face. She'd been staring. She'd never been in the same room with Native Americans before. Their dark skin and long, braided hair surprised her. She'd never seen anyone who looked like this in Chicago.

Ed Eagle Plume chuckled. "So this is the new housekeeper. Where've you been hidin' her all these years?"

Buck looked squarely into Ellie's green eyes and uttered a polite, "Pleased to meet you, Miss Parker."

Ellie responded shyly, then sat down in her accustomed place. The men sat down after her. She started to reach for the platter of chicken when Ben's voice stopped her short. "Ed, would you ask the blessin'?"

Ellie did more staring as the three men bowed their heads. Embarrassed, she dropped her gaze. She wondered why all of a sudden they were having a prayer before the meal. It made her uncomfortable. Buck Eagle Plume made Ellie even more uncomfortable. She'd been in the presence of good looking guys before, but none of them ever stirred her emotions as this one did. Buck was different. His features were sharp, clean cut as if they'd been chiseled from granite. His skin was not as dark as his grandfather's, and his eyes were more brown than black. There was a ruggedness and strength about him that left Ellie feeling overwhelmed. She found it hard to meet his eyes.

Ed broke the awkward silence. "Why, Miss Parker, I do believe this is the finest fried chicken I've ever eaten."

Ben chimed in. "And those potatoes . . . They'll really stick with a fella."

The two older men were obviously trying to make Ellie feel better. Buck's lack of comment told her the unvarnished truth. He grinned when he noticed the fresh bandages on two of her fingers. From then on Ellie tried to keep her hands under the table as much as possible. She hoped Mr. Buck Whatshisname might choke on a bone. Ellie sighed in relief when the tortuous meal finally came to an end because she was emotionally drained. If this was an indication of how her summer was going to go, she was in real trouble. The men got up to leave. Ellie followed them to the door. Mr. Eagle Plume reached out to shake her hand. "It's been a real pleasure meetin' you, Miss Parker."

Ellie liked him. She gave him a charming smile. "Please, call me Ellie. My friends call me Ellie."

"All right, Ellie. I hope we'll be seeing more of you." Ed followed Ben out the door.

Buck was the last to leave. Ellie stepped away from him self-consciously. Buck looked through her, his brown eyes unreadable as he tipped his hat to her. "Goodbye . . . Miss Parker."

Ornery Bronc

SAM HURRIED without appearing to be in a hurry, moving easily among the horses. He caught several geldings and tied them to the hitching rail. His hands moved in quick, smooth strokes as he brushed their new summer coats to a high sheen. He was proud of these colts, and today he wanted them to look their best. He knew Ben Magruder thought highly of the Eagle Plumes. He was hoping they would buy one of the geldings. Ben had given Sam special instructions to pull only the finest horses out of the herd to show them. And now, standing before Sam were five of the finest Quarter Horse geldings a man could ever hope to see.

He tipped his hat back on his head and spoke fondly to his charges. "Well, boys, this is it. You behave and show how smart you are, and one of you'll end up with a real fine home."

Sam's final inspection was interrupted by the sound of approaching voices. He looked up from the hoof he was cleaning to see his boss coming down the hill with two men. He sized up the visitors with the same professional eye he

Buck and the Blue Roan

would a horse. Sam liked what he saw. He classed Ed Eagle Plume in with Ben Magruder and Gordon Ritter: all three old time, honest Montana ranchers. Something about the youngest of the three men caused Sam to take a second, closer look. It was the face. The angular jaw was framed by jet black braided hair. An almost grin teased his mouth, and his brown eyes danced with mischief as if he had a private secret. The forehead was high and broad, showing his Flathead heritage. Even thought it was a young face, it showed a strength that would become more apparent with age.

Ben's hearty greeting broke off Sam's reflections. Ben made introductions all around and then he got right to the point. "Fellas, standin' before you is the result of years of careful breedin' and herd management. I've put the best years of my life into these horses. What do you think?"

There were several minutes of silence while Ed and Buck examined the five geldings. They walked around them slowly, taking time to notice important details such as length of hip, depth of girth, angle of the shoulder and pastern; all important details when choosing an animal to stand up under the stress of competitive roping.

Ed walked up to one of the geldings, a stout bay. "Let's put a saddle on this one. I'd like to see him work."

Sam untied the bay and led him to the barn. He stopped outside the tack room and dropped the gelding's lead rope. The gelding never moved from the spot where Sam left him. Sam knew that a horse that could be ground tied like that was the most desirable. After the gelding had been saddled,

Sam took him to the arena. He rode him easy, letting him warm up. Then he backed him into the roping box while Ben loaded a calf in the chute. The gelding stood quietly until Ben released the calf. Sam positioned the colt behind the calf and let him lope after the calf to the end of the arena. The colt performed flawlessly.

Ed nodded his approval and said, "Look at the way that colt watches cattle. He never took his eyes off that calf. I like his style."

The rest of the geldings were saddled and ridden. Buck tried them all after Sam was finished. He said he was pleased with how well they were started.

It was around three p.m. when Buck handed the reins of the last horse back to Sam. He looked at the horse trainer with admiration. "These colts have a nice handle on them. Maybe someday I can learn some of your secrets."

Sam liked this young cowboy from the Flathead Valley. "Maybe
. . . someday."

Ed looked at his watch. "It's time to be headin' back, so let's get down to business. Which one of these outlaw broncs do you want to take home?"

Buck looked at the geldings one last time. He went over their individual strengths and weaknesses. There was no doubt which one he liked best. "They're all good, but the bay's my pick."

Ed smiled his approval. "He's my choice, too. I'll settle with Ben, and then we'll load him and head home."

"Okay, Grandfather. I'll just look around a bit until you're ready to go."

Ben and Ed went to the ranch house to settle the purchase of the bay gelding. While Sam was putting the other geldings back in their stalls, Buck walked over to the large holding corral. He leaned against the rough poles and watched the horses milling around inside. Gloom settled over Buck in a thick cloud. He knew he should be feeling excited about the new horse, but he couldn't. There was no doubt about the gelding's quality, yet something was missing. He lacked that something special that makes certain horses stand out above the rest. Horsemen called it "presence," or "the look of the eagle." To Buck, it was the kind of pride and self-confidence that gave a horse an extra edge in competition.

Suddenly, a commotion inside the corral attracted Buck's attention. There was an angry squeal, followed by the dull thud of hooves on flesh. The herd parted to give the attacker ample room. In the middle of the corral stood a proud, defiant, stocky, blue roan mare. Buck straightened up to get a better look at her. His movement caught her attention. She watched him and snorted in distrust. Buck took his hat off and slapped it against his thigh. The blue roan mare exploded into action. She did a one-eighty-degree spin, shot to the far side of the corral, then turned to face Buck, her eyes white-rimmed, and nostrils dilated to suck in his scent.

A whistle of surprise and admiration escaped Buck's lips. "You move like a mountain lion, and I bet you're twice as friendly."

"You want to stay clear of that horse."

Buck turned to see Sam standing behind him. "She sure can move. How come she wasn't with the others?"

Sam's serious expression backed his words. "That blue mare's going to end up in someone's buckin' string or as a sack of dog food. I've yet to be able to stick with her for more than three jumps. The only reason I keep tryin' is because she's out of the boss's champion mare."

Buck knew of Sam's reputation as a rider and that not many horses were able to throw him. "She's tough?"

"Tough isn't the word for it. She's just a plain mean, ornery bronc."

"But Sam, look at the way she holds herself. She's got the look of the eagle."

"Now kid, don't go getting' starry-eyed over that horse. Take my advice and forget you ever saw her."

In spite of Sam's advice, Buck couldn't forget the blue roan mare. He thought of her all the way home and for several days afterward. His logic told him Sam was right. He didn't want a mare, and he certainly didn't need to take on a bronc. Besides, he had a good horse in the new bay gelding. Still, Buck couldn't get the picture of the proud head, the wild eyes and the sleek blue hair coat out of his mind. He figured the mare to be the type of horse that would never join up with humans; she might be conditioned to tolerate them, but she would never give herself completely.

♦♦♦

The brooding young cowboy from the Flathead Valley wasn't the only one carrying on a mental debate. Since the moment Buck Eagle Plume walked out the front door of Ben's house, Ellie had been in a state of emotional turmoil. One moment she liked him. He was so good looking and polite. The next moment she hated him. He was too sure of himself—smug, cocky; like he thought he was better than her. His "goodbye, Miss Parker" really irked her. He couldn't be much older than she was, yet he treated her like a child. Who did he think he was? Most of the time she tried to convince herself she really didn't care. Why let herself get all worked up over some hick cowboy anyway?

"Is somethin' ailin' you, Ellie?" Ben said.

Ellie sat daydreaming. Ben asked her again. Her face turned red when she realized she'd revealed her emotions. "No . . . no, I'm feeling fine. Uncle Ben, have you known the Eagle Plumes a long time?"

"Why, yes. I've known Ed about thirty years. Why do you ask?"

"Oh, I was just curious. There's one thing I was wondering. Why did we say grace at lunch the other day when they were here?"

"It's their custom. They've been church goin' folks for as long as I can remember. Most of the Native Americans in

Montana went to Catholic schools because that was all they could do on the Reservation. Many of them are returning to their traditional religious practices now, but Ed still practices his Catholic faith."

"Do they really believe all that stuff about gods and spirits?"

"Well, it's a bit more complicated than that, but yes, they do. I've seen their beliefs pull them through some pretty rough times."

Ellie lapsed into silence, contemplating this new aspect of Buck Eagle Plume. Religion made her nervous, especially when people took it too seriously. She began to hope she would never see him again. Besides, she had a bigger problem because Ben didn't seem to drink alcohol. There wasn't even a beer in the house, and Ellie was beginning to feel a tight squeeze of panic around her heart as she wondered where and when she would be able to get her next drink.

♦♦♦

Sam lay in the dirt of the horse training corral, cursing the blue roan mare. This was the second time she'd bucked him off this morning, and he was getting tired of it. He got painfully to his feet and brushed the dirt off his chaps. He spoke to the mare in disgust. "You sorry bronc. For ten bucks I'd shoot you. You're lucky the boss is so fond of you."

The blue roan mare eyed Sam suspiciously. She was ready for a fight, and Sam knew it. He dreaded the

Buck and the Blue Roan

punishment he was about to take, but he picked up the bridle reins and led the mare to the center of the corral. Standing close to the mare's left shoulder, he grabbed the cheek piece of the bridle and pulled her head around to him. With his other hand, he took hold of the mane and swung up into the saddle. His right foot barely cleared the mare's rump when she exploded into action. Like a rocket the mare shot straight into the air. Sam fought to gain the right stirrup. When she came down, Sam completely lost sight of her head. He had ridden dozens of bucking horses in his life, but none with as much power as this one. Each jump jarred his body, causing bright lights to go off in his head, but Sam was determined to ride the mare. His mind kept him on long after his body wanted to get off the back of the horse. The roan was just as determined not to be ridden.

As the fight continued, the mare became reckless. Her bucking was less calculating and more frantic. She made a desperately high leap. When she came down, she stumbled and fell. Sam felt the mare going, but he was too numb to react in time. He kicked his feet free of the stirrups as the full weight of the mare's body crashed down on his left leg. He heard and felt his bones breaking. The mare rolled off Sam's leg and scrambled to her feet. She staggered away from the downed rider to the far side of the corral. She stopped, head down, sides heaving, rivulets of sweat running down her legs.

Sam tried to focus on the mare. He knew he was badly hurt. He sat up gingerly, trying not to move his left leg. His vision blurred as he looked down and saw his boot heel where his toes should've been. A wave of nausea swept over him as he passed out.

Ben watched the battle going on in the round corral from the living room window, while he struggled with indecision. He had high hopes for the roan mare, but he couldn't make a performance champion out of a bucking horse. He was also concerned for Sam's safety. Sam had worked for him for twenty years and was a good friend. Ben did not like the idea of having a horse around that was bound to hurt someone sooner or later.

The mare went down so fast it took several seconds for Ben's mind to grasp what his eyes saw. When it did register, he reacted with amazing speed for his age and size. He cleared the front porch steps in a single leap and sprinted down the hill toward the round corral. Ben yelled to one of the hands to come with him as he passed the barn. He slowed to a walk as he approached the training corral. He didn't want to make matters worse by startling the mare. What Ben saw made his throat constrict and his heart pound. Sam lay sprawled in the dirt like a crumpled rag doll, his face smeared with blood from the nose bleed the mare's beating gave him.

Ben spoke quietly to the cowboy who had now reached his side. "I'm going in. When I get to Sam, you come in and get the mare out."

Ben went to the gate and eased it open. All of the time he kept up a non-stop monolog to keep the roan mare quiet.

The exhausted horse stood her ground and allowed the cowboy to take hold of the reins as Ben stood by Sam's side. The hired hand led the mare from the corral. As soon as they were safely out of the corral, Ben went into action. He called to one of the other hired men. "Go to the house and call an ambulance. And send Ellie down with some blankets."

Ben kneeled next to Sam to get a better look at his injuries. Sam's left leg caught his attention first. The lower leg was strangely distorted. The boot was facing backward. Ben crawled down to Sam's feet. He knew the main rule of first aid was never move a broken limb, but he figured this situation was an exception. The way the leg was twisted, the blood would be cut off to the foot. It would be at least thirty minutes before he would get to the hospital in Hamilton. By then the tissue damage below the break might cause Sam to lose his foot. Ben hoped Sam's chaps would give the leg a little extra support. He grasped the toe and the heel of the boot and gently rotated the foot back into its normal position. He heard a muffled choking sound behind him. Turning, he saw Ellie standing white-faced and trembling, blankets in her arms.

"Ellie, bring the blankets here." The authority in his voice kept her from losing control. She walked mechanically to Ben's side. He took the blankets and covered Sam. Sam's eyes fluttered open, and he vomited. Ben held Sam's head, so he would not choke and spoke to reassure him. "It's okay, Sam. You're going to be all right."

Sam smiled weakly. "I really did it good this time, didn't I?"

Ben nodded his head. "I'm afraid so."

"Who's going to finish breakin' those colts?" Sam's face twisted in pain, and sweat beaded on his pale forehead.

Ben's strained to hear the sound of an approaching ambulance. He put his big hand on his friend's shoulder. "Don't worry. Rest easy now. You're going to be all right." He said it more for himself than for Sam because he wasn't sure Sam *was* going to be "all right."

POINT OF NO RETURN

THE RINGING PHONE DEMANDED to be answered. Buck hurried. He took the porch steps two at a time, hoping whoever was calling would not hang up. He hated making a spectacular fifty-yard dash only to be greeted by a dial tone when he picked up the receiver. Buck's long stride took him into the kitchen. Out of breath, he lunged for the receiver. The wall phone gave what was probably its last ring.

"Hello?"

"Hello. Is this Buck?"

"Speaking."

"Ben Magruder here. It sounds like you had a bit of a run to the phone."

"A bit, but I'm used to it. What can I do for you, Mr. Magruder?"

"I was hopin' you could help me out. You remember Sam, my trainer? Well, he got busted up by the blue roan mare. He'll be laid up for the rest of the summer. I'd like to offer you the job of trainin' the rest of my colts."

Buck couldn't organize his thoughts fast enough to keep up with what he was hearing on the phone. After a long pause, Buck answered. "I'm sorry to hear about Sam. He seems like a good man. I'm not sure I heard you right. Did you want me to finish training your horses?"

"I sure do, if it's okay with your grandfather and he can do without you for the summer. Talk it over with him and let me know in a couple of days what you decide."

"I'll do that, Mr. Magruder. Thanks for callin'."

Buck hung up the receiver and went outside. He walked to the barn where he'd been headed before he was sidetracked by the phone. He got out the saddle soap and began cleaning his saddle. As Buck scrubbed the dirt out of his saddle, he thought about his conversation with Ben Magruder. The more he thought about it, the more he liked the idea of going to work for him. It was time for him to do something different. He needed a change.

That night at dinner, Buck told his grandfather about his phone conversation with Ben Magruder. There was silence for a moment while his grandfather finished eating. After swallowing, he cleared his throat. "What do you want to do?"

"I'd like to go to work for Mr. Magruder if you can spare me."

Ed gazed at Buck for a moment, then said, "If I said no, I know you'd respect my decision. You know I could use you here myself, but if you feel you need to go, then I suppose it's okay with me. We have enough help now. I can always hire some of your friends during haying. I think we can get along without you."

Buck didn't realize until that moment that he'd been holding his breath. He let it go with a sigh. "Thanks, Grandfather."

Then he turned to his brother. "How about you, Rusty? Will you miss your little brother if I go away for the summer?"

Rusty smiled sweetly at his brother. "Me go wi Bu?"

For the first time, Buck realized what an impact his decision to leave might have on his brother. They'd never been away from each other, not even for a night. "No, Rusty, you can't go with me this time. I won't be gone long, and I'll be back before you know it."

Rusty looked first at his grandfather and then at Buck. His confusion and hurt clouded his expression. "Me go wi Bu. Bu no leave Rusty."

Ed raised his eyebrows and shrugged when Buck looked to him for support. "This is your call. Your leaving will be hard on all of us, but it will be hardest on Rusty. Do what you have to. These kinds of choices always come with a price."

Buck took a long look into his grandfather's eyes. Was this supposed to be some sort of get-even remark or was it an excuse? As usual, his grandfather was unreadable. "Rusty, someone has been hurt. I have to help a friend. You can help too by staying here to take care of Grandfather and Miss Hextall."

♦♦♦

Ellie swung peacefully on the porch swing, looking out across the valley with a novel resting forgotten in her lap. The robins chirping in full song added to the beautiful spring evening. How different this was from the noise and confusion of the big city. Chicago . . . it was so distant and unreal to her now.

The screen door screeched in protest as Ben came out on the porch. "Mind if I join you?"

Ellie looked up, glad for his company. She was growing very fond of her Uncle Ben. "No, please, come sit down with me."

Ben sat next to her on the porch swing. "Beautiful evenin' isn't it?"

"Yes, it is." Ellie laughed softly, self-consciously. "Listen to me. I'm carrying on like some ancient philosopher. It must be the mountain air that's intoxicating me."

Ben's expression was gentle, almost reverent. "It's the greatness of the country that makes you feel these things. The power you feel . . . my wife used to say it was God."

"Uncle Ben, do you believe in God?"

"I don't know, Ellie . . . I just don't know."

They lapsed into silence, each one considering the implications of their conversation. Neither one of them could remember at what moment the soft twilight slipped into darkness. With the darkness came a chilling breeze. Ellie shivered. Her slight movement brought Ben back to the present. "We best go inside before we both catch pneumonia."

She smiled at the age-old exaggeration. "Okay, let's go in, and I'll fix us some hot chocolate."

"That sounds good to me."

Ben and Ellie sat at the kitchen table, drinking their hot cocoa, enjoying the lingering heat from the wood stove. Ben chuckled to himself. Ellie looked at him, an unspoken question forming on her lips.

"I plum forgot the reason I came out on the porch to talk to you. I found someone to fill in for Sam until he heals up."

Ellie was mildly curious. "That's nice, Uncle Ben."

"Well, don't you want to know who it is?"

Ellie figured she should humor him. "Who is it?"

Ben watched her closely, seeming to savor each moment of suspense. "Buck Eagle Plume."

Ellie froze, her hot chocolate halfway to her lips. "Who?"

Her reaction pleased Ben. "Remember your first cooking task—the Eagle Plumes from the Flathead Valley?"

Ellie got up, suddenly concerned with cleaning the table. She spoke under her breath. "How could I ever forget?" Then, changing the subject, "I better get to bed. I've got a lot of work to do tomorrow."

Ben spoke softly to her retreating back. "You better start shakin' out a loop, gal. They don't come any finer than Buck Eagle Plume."

♦♦♦

Buck finished loading his gear into his pickup. It didn't look like much: one suitcase, his saddle and his rope bag. He decided to take his horse trailer, too. He heard there was a good team-roping club in the Bitterroots, and he wanted to get in on as much roping as possible. He didn't feel right about asking Mr. Magruder for the use of his trailer. As for horses, he would have as many available to him as he could use.

Part of his job would be to give the three-year-olds experience with rope and cattle. None of them would be ready for serious competition, but with Chester gone, neither was he.

Buck made one last mental check of all the items he needed. He was ready to leave. He hated goodbyes, but he walked resolutely up the porch steps and into the kitchen. His grandfather sat at the table, sipping his morning coffee.

"Well, everything's loaded. I guess I'm ready to leave."

His grandfather cleared his throat, stood up and grasped Buck's hand in a firm handshake. "Take care, Buck. Give my regards to Ben."

For a moment, grandfather and grandson looked into each other's eyes, each wanting something from the other that could not be given. Ed let go and stepped back from Buck.

Rusty tugged on Buck's sleeve and sniffled. "Bu no go."

Buck embraced his brother, embarrassed by the emotion. "Now Rusty, don't cry. I'll be back before you know it. You look after Grandfather and Miss Hextall like we talked about."

Rusty managed a crooked smile in spite of his tears. "I miss you, Bu."

Ed came to Buck's rescue. "It looks like a beautiful day for a drive. Have a safe trip down."

Buck tipped his hat to Miss Hextall and turned to leave. She touched his arm gently. "Don't worry, Buck. I'll take good care of them while you're gone."

"Thanks. You don't know how much that means to me." As Buck walked down the path to his truck, he wondered if this was how his mother had felt the day his dad left for the Middle East. Vietnam, Iraq: these were distant lands that had robbed him of his grandfather and his father's love.

♦♦♦

Ellie tried to shut out the persistent ringing of the alarm clock. Old habits were hard to break. She still was not used to getting up at five-thirty. That was why she put the alarm on the dresser instead of on the nightstand next to the bed. If it were near her, she would simply shut it off and go back to sleep.

She groaned and stretched, reluctant to crawl out from under the warmth of the big quilt. The early summer mornings were still chilly, especially at this hour. Uncle Ben had been right. It was the best part of the day . . . once you got up.

"Oh, all right. I'm coming." Ellie got out of bed and went to the dresser to silence the clock.

The early morning sun shone through the kitchen window, giving the room a warm, friendly glow and the promise of a glorious day. Ellie enjoyed getting breakfast; the aroma of fresh perked coffee and muffins in the oven gave her a real sense of accomplishment. She smiled to herself. If only her friends could see her now. Most of them either drank or smoked their breakfast.

"Good mornin', Ellie." Uncle Ben came in and sat in his accustomed spot.

"Good morning, Uncle Ben." Ellie brought a steaming mug of coffee over to the table and put it down in front of Ben. Next came the scrambled eggs, the bacon and the muffins. For a time, the kitchen was silent as Ben and Ellie enjoyed their breakfast. Ellie smiled to herself, glad that she had finally gone to the camp cook and asked for his help. It had worked out well in more ways than she hoped. The cook liked his beer, and he kept several cases in the storeroom for himself and the men. There were always six-packs in the meat cooler, and nobody seemed to keep track of them. She'd been able to sneak several cans without making a noticeable dent in the supply.

Ben looked up from his plate. "Gal, you sure are getting' to be a good cook. You'll make a fine wife someday. Oh, that reminds me, Buck Eagle Plume should be comin' in sometime this mornin'."

Ellie looked at her uncle in horror. Surely he wasn't thinking of trying to pair her up with Buck. No, he had a lot of things on his mind. It was probably just an overreaction on her part. But then, why should she react at all to the arrival of Buck Eagle Plume? He was just another hired hand.

"Uncle Ben, where will Mr. Eagle Plume be staying while he's here?"

Ben struggled to keep from laughing. "'*Mr. Eagle Plume'* will be eatin' and sleepin' with the other hands. But since he's a friend of the family, you can invite him to the house for Sunday dinners if you'd like."

"Oh, no, I don't want him up here. No, that's not what I mean . . . I mean, I was just wondering where he was going to stay . . . in case I had to make up a bed for him or something." It was a poor cover up, and Ellie knew it. Her face flushed.

Ben seemed to be enjoying the conversation. "I meant what I said about havin' him up for Sunday dinners. Buck's a friend. I'd like to get to know him better."

"You're right, Uncle Ben. I'm sorry for the way that sounded." Maybe she had been too hard on "Mr. Eagle Plume." It might be nice to have someone her own age to talk to again. Ellie started rushing around clearing the table. Ben had to rescue his half-full coffee mug before she could whisk it off to the sink.

Ellie blushed again as she caught him grinning like the Joker.

♦♦♦

Buck felt the way he did before his first rodeo performance. The pit of his stomach was tight and cold with anticipation. It was hard saying goodbye to his family, but now that the Flathead Valley was behind him, he was looking forward with eagerness to the challenge ahead. He wondered if the blue roan mare would be a part of that challenge. Buck hoped so. He had been trying to forget her, but pictures of her kept filtering back into his mind. It was mid-morning when he pulled into the Magruder ranch. Ben met him down by the bunkhouse. Buck parked his truck and trailer where Ben indicated. As soon as he got out of the truck, his hand was grasped in the famous Magruder squeeze.

"Buck, it's good to have you here."

"It's good to be here, Mr. Magruder."

"Please, call me Ben. It makes me feel old bein' called Mr. Magruder.

"I'll give it a try, Ben." Buck felt awkward calling his boss by his first name.

"That's better. Now, let's get you settled. Then I'll show you around and explain the routine."

"Sounds good to me. I've been lookin' forward to workin' with the three-year-olds, especially the blue roan."

A cloud of emotion passed over Ben's face. "I'm afraid you won't get that chance. I'm havin' you take a load of canners to the sale next week. The blue roan is goin' with them."

Buck's stomach knotted. The idea of the blue roan mare going to slaughter sickened him, even though Ben was right. Without giving it any more thought, he knew he had

Buck and the Blue Roan

to have her, at any price. "Please, Ben, let me try her. I know I can train her. I'd like to buy her from you."

"Buck, that horse in no good. You know what she did to Sam. Next time she may kill someone. I won't give her that chance. As for buying her, I won't sell a horse like that as a riding horse. If you think you want her that bad, you'll have to buy her at the sale."

Buck walked a fine line. He didn't want to offend Ben, but he knew he had to have the mare. "Would you mind if I buy her?"

Ben could see the longing in Buck's eyes. He admired his determination. A few years earlier he might have wanted to tackle the blue roan himself. "I'd advise against it, but if you're dead set on getting her, I won't stop you."

"Thank you, Mr. Magruder." Buck felt a great load being lifted off his shoulders, but he didn't know why. For some reason, he couldn't put a finger on why he felt drawn to the blue roan.

He spent the remaining time before lunch getting settled in the bunkhouse. When the cook rang the bell for the noon meal, Ben went with him to the cook shack to introduce him to the rest of the crew.

Buck was the youngest man there, but he felt right at home. The faces he saw around the table were open and honest. Soon they would be the faces of friends.

"Well, Buck, I better get on up to the house before Ellie feeds my lunch to the dog. I'll meet you down at the barn at one."

"I'll be there."

Buck sat down at the table and started dishing up his lunch from platters of food in front of him. One thing was for sure, he wouldn't starve as long as he was working for this outfit. The food was plentiful and tasty. The noon meal passed in conversation about the weather, cattle prices and what the hay crop was looking like. Occasionally, the men would question Buck about his home and family. The atmosphere was pleasant. Any nervousness he felt was washed away by the easy talking of the men.

Buck was grateful to Ben for giving him a chance to get out on his own. He thought of Ben living alone up in the big house and wondered if he was hurting, too. Then he remembered . . . Ben wasn't alone. Miss Parker was spending the summer. Now there was someone he hadn't thought much about. He grinned to himself. She sure wasn't much of a cook, but she was pretty even with the hardware in her lip. The sound of chairs being pushed back brought Buck out of his reflections. It was almost one: time to go to work. The hands began leaving the cook shack to return to their various jobs.

Buck shook hands with the cook. "Thanks. I can tell eatin' is goin' to be the highlight of my day around here."

The cook grinned. "It's nice to have someone around with a taste for the finer things in life."

Buck left the cook shack and headed for the barn. He'd committed himself to staying; there was no turning back now. He thought of Rusty and knew he would miss his brother, but he also trusted Miss Hextall to keep her word. If only his mother hadn't . . .

Sold

THE MORNING DRAGGED ON endlessly as Ellie tried, without success, to keep occupied. She didn't like being at the mercy of her emotions, but she couldn't keep Buck Eagle Plume off her mind. It had been several weeks since his arrival, and he'd never come to the house in spite of Ben's numerous invitations.

She was bored and tired of being treated like a maid. She looked at her hands dripping with dish water. They were wrinkled, and her nails were broken. She needed a drink. It was times like this when she really missed her smartphone. She put the last dish in the rack and went outside. There were still more chores ahead of her, so she went to the garden.

The day grew hot as the morning progressed. Ellie straightened up, rubbing her aching lower back. The effort of weeding had momentarily taken her mind off Buck.

She looked at her watch—almost eleven. It was time to clean up before she started fixing Uncle Ben's lunch. The sound of an approaching vehicle turned her attention once again to the driveway. A dark, metallic blue pickup and horse trailer pulled up the driveway. She figured Buck was coming back from town. Ellie fought down the desire to make a run for the house. She was a mess of dirt and perspiration. She forced herself to get up and walk in a slow, dignified manner without looking in the direction of the driveway again.

Once in the house, she began to fret. Where was Uncle Ben? If he didn't come soon, his sandwiches would dry out. Ellie was running out of things to do. She thought longingly of the beer cans she'd hidden in the haystack behind the barn. Ellie needed a drink to calm her trembling hands, and she was dying to find out what Uncle Ben had to say about Buck's work. Her impatience was rewarded by the sound of the back door opening.

Ben came in and sat down at the kitchen table. He smiled innocently at Ellie. "How did your mornin' go?"

Ellie smiled back sweetly, too sweetly. "The garden is a hell hole. Weeding sucks! How was your morning?"

Ben ignored her tone. "Busy. I checked on the hay. It'll be ready to cut after the 4th of July. It's a good crop this year. All the rain we've had this spring has sure helped."

Ellie was getting exasperated. She knew Uncle Ben knew what she was after. She also knew he would make her work for any information he had about Buck. Sometimes men could be impossible! Well, she could play that game, too. Pride wouldn't allow her to come right out and ask. What did she care about Buck Eagle Plume anyway?

"Uncle Ben, do you know what I'd really like to do?"

"What would you really like to do?"

"I'd like to learn how to ride a horse."

"But you said you thought horses were smelly and gross. What's changed?"

Ellie fumbled with an excuse. "Well, maybe I was tired when I said that. So can I?"

Ben gave her a knowing look. "I think that can be arranged, and I know just the person to teach you. I imagine he'll have time."

Ellie wasn't prepared for this turn of events. "But I thought *you* would teach me."

Ben looked apologetic. "Runnin' this ranch takes up most of my time. Come evenin' I'm too tired to be much of a teacher. I'm not as young as I used to be. Besides, it's about time you and Buck got to know each other."

Ellie started to protest, but then she changed her mind. She wanted to ride a horse in the worst way. There was no sense in ruining her chances to get out and away from all the house work. "Could we find a horse for me to ride this evening?

Ben smiled warmly. "I don't see why not."

♦♦♦

Buck sat on a bale of hay waiting for Ben to come to the barn. He chewed tentatively on a long piece of Timothy grass. A tiny seed of homesickness was sprouting in his heart. He hoped he wasn't putting a strain on his grandfather's workload by leaving. Maybe he shouldn't have taken this job. He wasn't sure he wanted to be alone with himself. At least at home, he could talk to Rusty even though he knew his brother couldn't understand, but it helped just to vent his frustration. He knew there wasn't anyone around here he could feel comfortable sharing his feelings with. "Man, what have I gotten myself into?"

Ben came into the barn whistling a cheerful tune. Buck stood up to meet him, hoping Ben hadn't heard him talking to himself. "I'm ready for my orders, boss."

Ben grinned. Sam had been the only hand he had who called him "boss." It was good to hear it again. "Your main responsibility will be working with the young horses. You'll be usin' them to check on the cattle and to take salt to the salt licks. I've some leased land across the river, so you'll have a chance to give them some time in the trailer, too. You'll also be responsible for the cleanin' and repairin' of the tack. There'll be times when I'll have you run into town on ranch business. Your evenin's and weekends are your own. Any questions?"

After that list, Buck hesitated to ask, but he figured he better find out what he had to deal with. "Will I be doin' any fencin' or hayin'?"

"Only in case of emergency. We have to save your strength for those young horses. Ben was half-serious, half-joking. "I do have one favor to ask of you, though."

Buck was so pleased with not having to do the haying that he felt ready to do anything for Ben. "Sure, I'll help in any way I can."

"Ellie's been beggin' me to teach her to ride. Frankly, I just don't have the time. I was wonderin' if you could give her a few lessons. It would tie up your evenin's for a bit, but I'd be willin' to pay you extra."

Buck stood speechless. Moments earlier he'd been filled with such gratitude he was willing to make any kind of heroic sacrifice for Ben's sake. But this . . . to have to babysit some spoiled city girl in his spare time . . . this was going beyond heroic. However, he knew he could never turn Ben down. "I'll do it if it will help you out."

"Thanks. I really appreciate you doin' this for me. After supper why don't you come down to the wranglin' pasture with Ellie and me, and we'll pick out a nice gentle horse for her?"

"I'll be there."

Buck figured he owed Ben this favor. He resigned himself to the fact that he'd be tied down for a while to Ellie. He'd make the best of it. Maybe he'd get lucky, and she'd decide she didn't like horses after all.

Buck spent the rest of the day familiarizing himself with the ranch. He shoveled out the stalls in the barn, filled the water troughs and straightened up the tack room. Tomorrow was Saturday. He decided he'd work with some of the colts, just to get them used to him. Then he'd ask Ben where the team ropers met for practice. He was anxious to meet the neighbors and to start roping again.

♦♦♦

Ellie felt like she'd been in a wreck, and her nerves were strung tighter than piano wire. She was excited about learning to ride and a little bit scared. Horses were so big. To make this new experience more stressful, Uncle Ben had asked Buck Eagle Plume to do the teaching. She wasn't thoroughly convinced her uncle was as busy as he made out to be, but she'd no choice other than to go along with him. If she wanted to learn to ride, she would have to learn from Buck.

She breathed deeply to try to calm the nerves that knotted her stomach as she and Ben walked down to the wrangling pasture. Ellie knew her sick feeling wasn't caused by anything she'd eaten because she'd been too excited to eat much at dinner. The feeling was familiar. She'd had it on her first date, and she got it every time she had to give a speech in class. Only this was worse. She hoped she didn't throw up.

Ben peered at Ellie. "You feelin' all right, gal? You look a little pale."

Ellie managed a weak smile. "I'm okay. Just a little nervous I guess."

Buck stood waiting for them. He was leaning on the fence watching the wrangling horses in the pasture. Ellie tried not to look at him and focused her attention on the horses.

Buck stepped in front of her and tipped his hat. "Evenin', Miss Parker."

"Whatever." Ellie quickly turned away, afraid her face would betray her emotions and took Ben's arm. "Are these the horses I can ride?"

"They sure are. Some of the bigger ones we use as packhorses. You don't want to ride them. They're too rough gaited, but look the others over and pick one out."

Ellie wasn't sure what "too rough gaited" meant, but just the size of the packhorses was enough to discourage her. For a moment she forgot Buck's presence as she got caught up in choosing a horse. A black and white paint was the first one to attract her attention. It reminded Ellie of the Indian stories she'd read as a little girl. Then there was a black horse—more memories of shining black stallions. Ellie drifted between her childhood fantasies and the real horses in front of her.

Ben's voice broke the spell. "Well, do you see any you like?"

Ellie was unsure. "They're all so beautiful. I can't make up my mind."

Buck, who had been watching Ellie as she looked over the horses, said, "May I make a suggestion?"

Ellie looked at Buck in surprise. She'd almost forgotten him. "Whatever."

"I think the buckskin over there would suit you. He's not real big, and he looks strong. He has a kind, gentle eye, and I'd guess he's up in years. He won't be tryin' any tricks with you."

Ben, nodded his approval. "I agree with Buck. He'd be a real good horse for you, Ellie. He's seen a few years and even more miles. He'll take good care of you."

Ellie looked skeptically at the buckskin gelding. "I hope he's not too old. I want a horse with some fire."

Ellie caught the slightest grin on Buck's face.

"If I may say so," Buck said, "you're better off startin' out with a quiet, older horse. You wouldn't expect to get on a motorcycle and ride it if you'd never learned to ride a bicycle, would you? Well, it's the same with a horse. You start out slow and work your way up as your ridin' improves."

There was a flash of fire in Ellie's green eyes, and Ben stepped in before things got out of hand. "He's right, Ellie. The buckskin will be a good horse for you. We'll give you somethin' with a little more pep when you're ready."

Ellie tried to control her anger. Buck treated her like a little kid, and so did Uncle Ben. She looked at the buckskin again. She was sure she wouldn't like the horse, but she gave in because she had no argument to offer. "Sure. Why not?"

♦♦♦

It was Monday morning, and the livestock auction would be starting in Missoula around nine o'clock. Buck backed the stock truck up to the loading chutes to load the horses going to the sale. Ben was sending some mares that were too old to raise foals, a crippled old pack gelding and the blue roan.

When the truck was in position, Buck went into the corral behind the loading chutes and ran the horses up the ramp and into the truck. The blue roan shied away from the loading ramp and ran past Buck. He made several unsuccessful attempts to load her. Buck was getting exasperated. "If you keep this up, you're going to end up in a dog food can for sure, sis."

He wasn't about to let a stubborn horse ruin his day, so he went to the tack room and got his rope out of his rope bag. Buck returned to the corral behind the loading chute. The blue mare eyed him wickedly as he shook out the loop and began swinging his rope over his head; then she panicked and raced around the corral at suicidal speed. The loading ramp promised escape. The mare thundered up the ramp and crashed into the horses in the truck. For a moment, the truck rattled and shook as the horses rearranged themselves to make room for the roan. The mare glared at Buck over the backs of the other horses. He shook his head, wondering why he wanted to buy her. "I see you're real fond of ropes, too."

♦♦♦

Ellie didn't say much to Ben as she served his breakfast. She still nursed her hurt feelings from the night before. She was mad because Ben had sided with Buck in choosing a horse for her to ride, and it was a blow to her pride. They seemed to forget she was almost a grown woman, capable of making her own decisions. Her mother was right when she told her men would try to control every situation they could. Ben and Buck had proved this theory last night.

Looking up from his breakfast plate, Ben seemed to sense her mood. "You about out of groceries?" he asked.

"We're low on coffee and flour. There're a few other baking things I need, too."

"How would you like to make a trip to town today?"

Ellie's face brightened. She'd love a quiet day by herself to do some shopping. "That sounds good to me. I need to get some things for myself, especially a pair of boots."

"Good. You can ride in with Buck. He's takin' a load of horses to the sale. No sense in makin' two trips to town. You don't need to worry about lunch. I'll eat with the crew. You best hurry. Buck'll have the truck loaded and ready to go in a few minutes."

Ben was out the door before Ellie could say a word. She swore silently at his retreating back. So much for her quiet day in town. Well, she may have to ride with Buck, but she didn't have to talk to him. She was tempted to make him wait for her. However, she'd been around the ranch long enough to know you didn't fool around when it came to ranch business. Instead, Ellie made up a list of grocery items, spent a little longer than necessary in front of the mirror, grabbed her purse and headed out the door.

It was a perfect morning. She inhaled the sweet mountain air tinged with hints of pine, cottonwood, damp earth and wild roses. She never dreamed air could smell so good. Her dark mood melted beneath the brilliance of the morning sun. This might not be such a bad day after all.

Ellie took her time walking from the house to the barn. As she neared the corrals, she spotted the stock truck with Buck leaning against the driver's side. She couldn't help grinning to herself. The grim expression on Buck's face told her he was just as thrilled about spending the day together as she was. Her resolution to keep silent faded away as the impish idea of tormenting him with conversation entered her head.

Ellie walked past him and flipped her thick hair away from her eyes coyly. "Good morning, Buck. It's a beautiful day isn't it?"

Buck tipped his hat in his usual way, being coolly polite. "Good morning. You're right. It is a beautiful day."

Ellie climbed into the cab of the stock truck. She'd never been in a big truck before, and her excitement at the prospect of a new adventure made her momentarily forget her plans for Buck. She was filled with questions, but she found herself feeling unexpectedly shy in the closeness of the cab. The big truck rumbled down the gravel road and onto Highway 93. Buck remained silent.

Ellie finally worked up enough courage to speak and asked the obvious question even though she already knew the answer. "Where are you taking the horses?"

"To the sale."

"What's going to happen to them?"

"They'll most likely go to the canner."

Ellie may have been a city girl, but she'd read enough horse stories to know what a canner was. She was horrified to think Uncle Ben would do that to his horses. "How awful!"

Buck saw the pain in Ellie's face. "I know it seems hard, but your uncle raises these horses as a business. He'd go broke if he carried every old horse on the place until it died. It's not pleasant, but it's a hard fact of ranch life."

Ellie considered Buck's answer and decided she didn't like its implications. "Is that what happens to all ranch horses?"

"No. Sometimes special horses are put down and buried on the place."

Something in the sound of Buck's voice caused Ellie to look at him. He sounded so sad. Buck turned his head briefly to look at her, and the hurt in his eyes caused her to drop her gaze. She felt as if she'd invaded something private in Buck's life. They lapsed into silence.

Ellie wondered about the pain she'd seen in Buck's brown eyes and decided not to ask any more questions for a while.

Buck drove through town to the stockyards. They unloaded the horses, and Buck filled out the necessary papers for their sale. When that was done, they joined the other buyers and sellers at the sale ring. Buck found two seats in the buyer's section and sat down. He turned to Ellie. "Now, you just sit on your hands and don't move until we leave. I don't want to end up takin' more horses home than we brought."

Ellie nodded, only half hearing what Buck said. She was caught up in the sights and sounds of the auction. The room was beginning to fill with cigarette smoke. She was surrounded by small groups of men who were in deep discussion about prices, weather and the state of the nation. The men were mostly older, wearing faded jeans or overalls. They seemed to be enjoying themselves. It was apparent to Ellie that the auction was a social event of sorts where men could come to exchange bits of news and get away to relax.

She also noticed there weren't many women in the crowd. Some of the men looked at her with mild curiosity, but Ellie didn't find them starring offensively. Western men seemed to think more of fine cattle and horses than they did of women. She found it refreshing, yet disturbing. She didn't like the idea of playing second fiddle to a cow. A few of the men recognized Buck and spoke to him in passing. Ellie was amazed how many of the men he knew, considering he'd only been in the valley a short time.

The auction started, and Ellie became thoroughly confused. She couldn't understand a word the auctioneer was saying. Animals were whisked in and out of the ring so fast she couldn't keep track of them. She never could tell for what price the animal sold. Ellie wanted to ask Buck, but she was afraid to show her ignorance. No use lowering his opinion of her any more than it already was.

Finally, Ellie looked at her watch. It was starting to get late. She wasn't sure why they were still sitting there. She began to squirm and fidget. Buck glared at her. She gave him an angry look, but she stopped her squirming. At that moment, a horse shot into the tiny sale ring. It slipped and almost fell on the sawdust covered floor. When it recovered, it stood frozen, shaking and dripping sweat. Its eyes were white-rimmed and wild with fear. Its nostrils wee dilated, showing red.

Everybody in the building seemed to hold their breath, momentarily shocked by the violent beauty of the horse. The auctioneer started up with his sale chant. The horse exploded, running, sliding and pivoting to escape collision with the high walls and fence. Ellie recognized Ben's blue roan mare. The horse made a frightening picture. Ellie was glad they were seated away from the fence.

The men buying canners bid on the mare, and Ellie went hot with anger. How could anybody kill a horse? It wasn't fair! Her heart went out to the wild looking horse. She became so involved with the plight of the blue roan mare, she wasn't aware Buck was bidding on the horse. The auctioneer finally said, "Going once. Going twice. Sold to the gentleman sitting next to the pretty gal."

Ellie turned and looked at Buck in amazement. She was so overcome with relief she almost hugged him. Instead, all she could do was say, "Oh, Buck, thank you." Then, embarrassed, she dropped her gaze.

They left the sale ring and went to the office to pay for the mare and collect the papers that went with the sale. When everything was in order, they went to the back pens to pick her up. This time the horse loaded in the stock truck without hesitation. Buck dropped the end gate behind her and sighed to himself. He turned to Ellie. "Well, let's go take care of your shoppin'."

Buck and the Blue Roan

Buck stayed in the truck while Ellie shopped. She finally returned with her purchases. Buck had to help her organize the front of the truck, so they could get everything in without squashing or breaking it. He grinned at the pile. "I sure hope you weren't plannin' on puttin' the groceries in back with the mare."

They then bought a week's supply of groceries and packed them in the truck cab along with the rest of Ellie's things. The ride home passed in silence. They were both tired, but Ellie was curious. Finally, she spoke. "Why did you do it?"

Buck was at a loss. "Do what?"

"Why did you buy the mare? I've heard Uncle Ben say she's dangerous and could never be a trustworthy saddle horse."

Buck kept silent for a few moments, thinking. He finally spoke. "There's something special about her. She's proud and . . . rebellious. I guess maybe we're two of a kind. I want to try to make somethin' of her, but I don't think she wants to be anything but to be left alone. She's a challenge, but there's hope if I can gain her trust."

For the second time that day, Buck surprised Ellie. Maybe there was more to him than she'd thought there was. He certainly didn't strike her as being rebellious. Ellie remained silent the rest of the ride home, lost in her thoughts. She'd have to watch Buck more closely from now on. He seemed to be hiding something, and she wanted to find out what it was.

Headin' and Heelin'

THE WARMTH OF THE MORNING SUN shining on his face woke Buck. The bunkhouse was empty except for a couple of hands sleeping off the effects of last night's trip to town. They snored loudly, their mouths open.

It was Saturday. Most of the men were gone for the weekend. Only the irrigators would be working. Buck yawned and stretched, rubbing the sleep from his eyes. He dressed quickly and went to the cook shack. The cook poured him a cup of steaming hot coffee and put a platter of cinnamon rolls on the table in front of him.

Buck savored the coffee. It was nice to be able to eat without the constant buzz of a room full of men around him. The rolls were good, almost as good as his grandfather's. He missed his family. Buck never realized how much he took them for granted until now. Tomorrow was Sunday. They'd be going to church. He wondered if it was just a habit with his grandfather, or if it really was an important part of his life. Buck's coffee went cold in his mug while his mind traveled miles away to the Flathead.

Buck and the Blue Roan

"You need a refill, Buck? 'The cook's voice startled Buck out of his thoughts.

"No, thanks. I better head out and do some work before the inclination wears off."

Buck went to the corral and caught several of the three-year-olds and tied them to the fence. One of them was the blue roan mare. He went to the tack room and got a brush and comb. Buck worked his way down the line of horses, brushing them, combing out their manes and tails and cleaning out the bottoms of their feet. He talked quietly to the young horses to get them used to his voice and build their confidence in him.

The blue mare was last in line. As Buck approached, she snorted and pulled back on the rope. When she found no slack, she threw a fit, thrashing around like a fish on the end of a line. Buck stood quietly and let her throw her tantrum. When she was through, he walked up to her and started brushing her. The mare's skin flinched at his touch. "You're a might nervy, sis."

Buck kept up a steady stream of monolog as he worked the mare over with the brush and comb. He was careful to stay close to her in case she decided to kick. He was in no hurry to end up like Sam. The mare never once relaxed her defensive attitude. Buck stroked the satin neck. "This is going to be a long, hard road, gal."

"Glad to see you two are getting' acquainted. "Buck turned at the sound of Ben's voice.

"Mornin', boss. Just thought I'd spend some time getting these colts used to me."

"That's good, but I hate to see you workin' so hard on your day off."

"Most of the time I don't consider handlin' horses work."

"I'm glad to hear you say that. By the way, will you have time for a lesson with Ellie this evenin'? She's feelin' too shy to ask you herself."

"Sure." Buck doubted Ellie was feeling shy. More likely, she was too stuck up to ask him. He'd seen the type before. Well, it didn't matter. He could put up with just about anything when he had to.

♦♦♦

Ellie busied herself clearing the supper dishes off the table. Her life at the Magruder ranch had slipped into a predictable routine. Only the guilt she felt stealing beer and the awkwardness she felt around Buck cast a shadow over an otherwise bearable summer, but most of the time she was able to push these feelings aside. She hummed quietly to herself as she went about her work.

"I'll take care of the dishes for you tonight. Buck's waitin' for you down at the corral." Ben went to the sink and started the dish water.

"What?" Ellie almost dropped the stack of dishes she was holding.

"Oh, didn't I tell you? I talked to Buck earlier this mornin'. He said he'd have time tonight to start your ridin' lessons."

"No, you didn't tell me."

"Well, you better hurry up and get your boots on. You don't want to keep him waitin'."

Ellie put the stack of dirty dishes in the sink and went to her room to put on her boots and new jeans. She smiled to herself. Uncle Ben was getting pretty obvious about his matchmaking. It was embarrassing, but she loved him for it. For his sake, she would play along with the game. It couldn't hurt anything. Buck Eagle Plume certainly wasn't a threat to her, and she'd be leaving in a few months anyway. For now, she would enjoy the pleasant Montana evening. No matter how hot it got during the day, it started cooling off by sunset.

Ellie went outside anticipating the coolness. A slight breeze lifted her hair off her shoulders. The last lingering rays of sunlight caught in the free blowing strands, making them shine like spun copper. She saw Buck at the barn and subconsciously hurried her steps.

When she drew near, Buck tipped his hat in his usual fashion. His voice was cool, distant. "Evenin'."

Buck's abrupt greeting hurt. Ellie hoped that after their day in town their relationship would be less formal. He seemed determined to keep her at arm's length. She answered lifelessly. "Good evening, Buck."

For a moment, there was an awkward silence between them, until Buck got down to the business at hand. "I brought in your horse. I'll show you how to catch and saddle him. I'll only show you once. From then on you're on your own. You'll remember things better that way."

Ellie could only nod in silent agreement. Somehow, this wasn't going the way she'd imagined it would.

Buck took a halter from the tack room and entered the holding corral where the horses were milling around. He approached the buckskin gelding, talking quietly to him the whole time. The gelding offered no resistance. Buck haltered him and led him out of the corral and tied him to the hitching rail.

Buck turned to Ellie. "When you're catchin' horses, the secret is to go in slow and talk to them. Never reach for their head, especially if the horse is not familiar with you. Approach their shoulder. Touch them there first. Then, put the lead rope around their neck before you put the halter on, so you have control of them if they try to pull away."

He then showed Ellie the proper way to groom and saddle a horse. "If you have any questions, ask them now. Tomorrow you'll be on your own."

Ellie remained silent. Her mind was in a whirl trying to take in the information Buck was giving her. She felt like she did when she was a little girl struggling to learn her multiplication tables for a demanding teacher.

Buck led the gelding around the corral. "Now, this is the correct way to get on your horse. While facin' the horse's tail, take the reins and a hunk of mane in your left hand. With your right hand, take the stirrup and twist around and put your left foot in it. Then grab the saddle horn with your right hand and swing up. Like this."

Buck mounted the gelding in one swift, fluid movement. It looked easy enough. "Now, you try it."

Buck and the Blue Roan

Ellie took the reins gingerly from Buck. She patted the buckskin on the neck, hoping he was as gentle as Uncle Ben said he was. She positioned herself as Buck had instructed her. All went well until she tried to get her foot in the stirrup. Try as she would, she couldn't get her leg high enough. Her jeans were embarrassingly tight. However, she wasn't about to make a fool of herself in front of Buck.

Ellie took a desperate lunging hop and jammed her foot in the stirrup. At the same time, she lost her grip on the saddle horn and her balance. For one desperate moment, she hopped around on her right leg before she fell in the dirt with her left foot caught in the stirrup . . . hanging. A cold wave of fear washed over Ellie. She'd heard stories of riders being dragged to death when they got hung up. She closed her eyes and waited for the gelding to bolt. Nothing happened. Ellie opened her eyes and looked around. The patient old gelding turned his head and looked at her with a knowing eye. Buck simply grinned. Ellie went hot with embarrassment. "Stupid horse."

Buck walked over to her, chuckling. "That was about the most interestin' mountin' method I've even seen." He reached out his hand to Ellie and helped her up and out of the stirrup. "Don't feel bad. Most cowboys don't get on their horses that way either."

Buck showed her an easier method of mounting. "Here, I'll help you this time. Take the reins and the horse's mane in your left hand and the cantle in your right hand, and I'll give you a boost."

Ellie did as she was told. Buck placed strong hands on her slender waist and practically lifted her into the saddle. Ellie's heart pounded. The ground looked so far away, but she was actually sitting on her first horse. She looked down at Buck with a reluctant grin. "How do I get down?"

"Just the reverse of how you got up."

"That's easy for you to say."

"Don't worry. I'll be here to catch you . . . if you fall." There was humor in Buck's eyes.

Ellie grimaced and began her dismount. Once again she felt the strong hands on her waist. When she reached the ground, she felt a little unsteady. Buck still had a hold of her. "I'm okay. You can take your hands off me now."

Buck let go, embarrassed. "You're welcome, Miss Parker."

Ellie sensed she'd crossed a line. Desperate not to lose the closeness of the moment, she tried to backtrack. "It's just I'm not used to having a man put his hands on me like that."

Buck studied her face and tried to judge her intent. "Okay, Ellie. I'll see you tomorrow night. We'll spend more time actually ridin'. And next time, wear some jeans that aren't so tight."

Ellie grinned sheepishly. "I will. Believe me, I will."

As Ellie walked slowly back to the house, the memory of Buck's strong hands on her waist made her heart pound. She felt things she didn't want to feel, and they scared her. She couldn't let this become more than a game. The last man she had loved had left her and her mom. She didn't want to feel that kind of pain ever again.

♦♦♦

Ben and Ellie sat on the old porch swing enjoying the quiet Sunday afternoon. It was starting to get hot, but a slight breeze teased them into staying outside. Ben looked up at the sky. "Not a cloud in sight. Looks like we can cut hay tomorrow."

Ellie brightened. "Can I help?"

Uncle Ben studied her for a moment. He guessed things were kind of slow for Ellie with only the two of them. "Sure, why not? You might build up some muscles on those skinny arms of yours."

Ellie grinned, a mischievous gleam in her eye as she threw him a line. "I hope so. I could use a little more meat on my bones. Besides, if I'm going to be a good rancher's wife, I better learn how to put up hay."

There was a long moment of silence before Ben cleared his throat to speak. He was about to rise to Ellie's bait when Buck's pickup drove in the driveway.

Ellie spoke up quickly. She wasn't about to let Ben have the last word on her this time. "Oh, look. There's Buck. Why don't' you ask him up for some ice tea and dessert?"

Ben sighed, a beaten man. "Well, I want to talk to him anyway." He stepped off the porch and motioned for Buck to come up to the house.

Ellie was glad she'd made a cake. This one wasn't from a box either. Ben had found his wife's old recipe file and given it to her. Ellie's cooking had been improving with practice. She hoped Buck liked chocolate cake. She watched him with appreciation as he walked up the gentle slope to the house. His striking appearance made it impossible not to enjoy looking at him. He wasn't very tall; she guessed around five ten, but he was lean and muscular. She couldn't picture him walking the halls of Oak Park High School where most of the boys were either thin and pale from playing non-stop video games or were gang bangers and stoners.

"Come sit a spell and have some dessert with us, Buck." Ben indicated a chair close by the swing.

"Thanks. Sounds good to me." Buck removed his hat and sat down.

Ellie rose and headed inside to fix their plates. As she rose, she caught Ben leaning over to Buck and overheard him say, "Her cookin's improved some since the last time you ate here."

Buck grinned but said nothing.

Ellie soon returned with a loaded tray.

"Here, Ellie, let me help you with that." Buck took the tray and put it on the pine box that served as the porch coffee table.

The gesture wasn't lost on Ben who eyed the young man with a smile. "Buck, one of the reasons I called you up here was to tell you there's a team ropin' practice at Gordon Ritter's this evenin'. I thought maybe we could all drive over, and I could introduce you to some of the other ropers."

Buck's face brightened. "I'd like to do that. What time?"

"We can leave here around five-thirty. That gives us time to get to Gordon's before they start ropin'."

Buck finished his cake and got up to leave. "I promised myself a ride this afternoon. I better get goin' Thanks for the cake, Ellie. It sure hit the spot."

He was off the porch and gone before Ellie could reply. She watched him go, perplexed by his haste. "Something's bothering Buck."

"How's that?"

"He was being nice to me. He didn't even tease me like he usually does."

Ben looked at Ellie and shook his head. "And here I thought you two were startin' to get along."

"Oh, Uncle Ben, you know what I mean."

"Nope. I'm afraid you lost me. Why do you think somethin's botherin' him?"

"He just seems far away. He was talking to us, but he really wasn't with us. It's just a hunch, but I think something is troubling him."

"Well, I didn't see it. But then, you women have a different way of lookin' at things. Whatever it is, he'll get over it."

"I hope so." Ellie felt uncomfortable with this serious side of Buck. She had enough problems of her own without getting involved with someone else's baggage.

♦♦♦

The drive to the Ritter ranch didn't take long. Ellie had mixed emotions about it. She enjoyed being close to Buck in the confines of Ben's pickup, but the lack of conversation made them all tense. Ben tried to keep things going with small talk but soon gave up. They made most of the trip in silence. The dark cloud hanging over Buck was almost tangible. It frightened her a little bit, but curiosity was getting the better of her.

Gordon's place was alive with activity when they arrived. A varied assortment of trucks, vans and trailers were parked in the field near the roping arena. There were men on horseback in the arena warming up. Some of the men were still saddling their horses, and some were bringing in the roping steers. It all looked very exciting to Ellie. She'd never seen roping before.

Ben found a place to park. "Come on, I'll introduce you to some of the fellas."

They walked through the men and horses, and Ben greeted friends and neighbors in his hearty way. He introduced Buck and Ellie as he went along.

Finally, Ben found who he was really looking for. "Gordon, I'd like you to meet my niece and my new horse trainer. Ellie Parker and Buck Eagle Plume. You remember Ed Eagle Plume from up in the Flathead? Well, Buck's his grandson."

"Sure, I remember Ed." Gordon reached out and gave Buck a firm handshake. "Pleased to meet ya, Buck." Then he turned to Ellie. "So, this is the gal who was causin' you sleepless nights?"

Gordon tipped his hat to Ellie. "The pleasure's mine, Miss Parker."

Ellie looked at Ben questioningly, but he seemed to be occupied with introducing Buck to another roper. She wondered what Gordon's remark had to do with her.

Buck's voice interrupted her thoughts. "Come on, Ellie. Let's go sit on the fence where we can get a good view of the action."

They walked to the arena and found a spot near the roping chutes. Buck made himself at home on the top rail. Ellie followed his example a bit awkwardly. She thought only birds perched on such small places. Evidently, cowboys did, too.

The steers were loaded in the chute. Several men straddled the chute, putting something on the steers' heads. "What are they doing?"

"They're puttin' horn wraps on the steers. It protects them from the rope."

"Buck, what exactly is heading and heeling?"

"Well, it all got started a long time ago, before there were corrals and chutes. Out on the open range there was no place to bring livestock for doctorin', so the cowboys came up with the method of headin' and heelin' the animal that needed doctorin'. One man, called the header, would rope the animal around the horns and drag it forward. At the same time, a second man, the heeler, would ride his horse in behind the animal and rope both if its back legs with his loop. Then they stretched it out until the steer fell on the ground. The horses were left to hold it until the doctorin' was done."

"Wow, that's dope! Do they still doctor their animals that way?"

"Not very often. Team ropin', like other rodeo events, is practiced mainly to keep the skill and the pride in the old ways alive. Besides that, it's just plain fun."

The loud clang of the chute gate opening drew their attention back to the arena. Ellie could see that any attempts at further conversation would be useless. Buck was totally absorbed in what was going on with the roping. For a while, she was, too. It looked exciting and possibly dangerous. However, not being able to appreciate the finer points of team roping, and afraid to ask, Ellie's attention began to wander.

She started watching the people around her. A cloud of dust shifted her attention to the driveway. A black van and a matching horse trailer sped up the lane. *Someone's late,* Ellie thought. She watched the approaching rig with interest. Whoever it was, they were making a showy entrance.

Buck interrupted her concentration. "Wow, would you look at that!"

Apparently, Ellie had missed something. "Look at what?"

"The run those two guys just made. It must've been around five seconds. I want to meet that header. It's been a long time since I've seen someone rope that good."

Again Ellie was at a loss. She couldn't tell a poor roper from an outstanding one, except the by number of misses. "What makes him so good?"

"Watch him and watch his horse. The horse puts him in a good throwin' position right by the steer's hip. When he catches, and I haven't seen him miss yet, he sets his steers and then logs them at a nice steady pace."

"That's nice." One day Ellie would ask Buck what "set" and "log" meant, but for now, she was more interested in the black van. She turned her attention back to the parking area. A dark-complexioned man got out and went to unload a horse from the trailer. His companion was a blond woman, who appeared to be not much older than herself. Ellie strained her eyes to catch all the details. She wished they hadn't parked so far away.

"What are you starin' at?" Once again, Buck frustrated her concentration. She was beginning to get annoyed.

"I'm not staring at anything. I am just wondering who those people in the van are."

Buck looked casually in the direction of the van. "I don't know. Why don't you ask Ben who they are?"

"That's exactly what I intend to do." Ellie started to climb down from her precarious perch. Her foot slipped on the rail. She half slid, half fell to the ground. Buck looked down at her and grinned. Ellie gave him a vicious glare, then stomped off to find Ben,

Buck watched her leave. "I wonder what's eatin' her."

BLACK WIDOW

IT DIDN'T TAKE ELLIE LONG to locate Ben. She found him talking to Gordon Ritter. She hesitated to break in on their conversation, so she stood a little off to the side until Ben soon noticed her.

"Well, what do you think of our western entertainment?" he said.

"It's sick." Just as Ellie was getting to learn the vernacular of cowboys and ranchers, she was pleased to see that Ben was getting familiar with her teenage terms.

"Maybe you'll be out there ropin' one of these days. Lots of women are good ropers."

Ellie grinned. After her first attempt at riding, she couldn't picture herself roping steers or anything else for that matter.

"I don't think so." She paused. "I was wondering, who are those people who just drove up in the van?"

Ben looking in the direction Ellie indicated. An expression of disgust crossed his face. "That's Eric Vance and Morgan Knight. You want to stay clear of them. They're the local low-life."

"What do you mean?"

"I mean, they're no good. Rumor has it that Vance is involved in some shady dealin's with livestock. I think he has a habit to support. No one's been able to prove it, though. Morgan Knight sticks to him like glue. She reminds me of a vulture, always feedin' off someone else's rotten scraps."

Gordon nodded in agreement. "You listen to your uncle, Miss Parker. Those two are pure poison. Eric Vance is as smooth as silk and twice as slippery. Morgan . . . well, she appears to be a regular Black Widow. I feel kind of sorry for her, though. She's too young to be hooked up with the likes of Vance."

"Thank you, Mr. Ritter. I'll stay away from them." Ellie thought the two men were probably exaggerating. Finally, there might be someone more exciting to hang out with than old men and stuck-up cowboys. She walked back to the fence where she left Buck. He was gone.

Buck soon forgot about Ellie's sudden departure as he continued to watch the roping. He climbed down from the fence and headed for the roping chutes. All of the ropers, except the two presently running a steer, were waiting their turn. Buck approached a tall rider on a good-looking gray horse. He extended his hand. "Hi. I'm Buck Eagle Plume. I want to tell you how much I admire your ropin'. It's been a long time since I've seen it done that good."

The rider sized Buck up with an experienced eye. Finally, he leaned over and took the offered hand. "Thanks. My name's Tom Ford. You're new in the valley, aren't you?"

"Ben Magruder hired me for the summer to work his colts. I haven't been here long."

"It appears you know a little about ropin'."

"I grew up with it. I did some ropin' for the high school rodeo team."

"A hot shot, huh? Which end of the steer do you rope?"

"The heels. I'm lookin' for a steady ropin' partner if one's available."

Tom was surprised by Buck's sudden approach, but he liked his style. "You got a horse here?"

"No, I lost mine to a twisted gut this spring. I'm sort of in between horses right now."

"Sorry to hear that. I'd like to see how you rope. Stay here, and I'll see if Gordon has a horse and rope you can borrow."

Buck watched as Tom rode off to look for Gordon. Tom sat his horse well. He was relaxed, but not sloppy. Buck guessed Tom was about ten years his senior. He was tall and muscular, without being heavy. Buck had seen humor and mischief in Tom's eyes. He suspected behind that mature face an experienced prankster lurked, waiting for some unsuspecting soul. He was a 'coyote,' one admired by Natives for his clever wiles. Buck looked forward to getting better acquainted with this cowboy.

Tom soon returned, leading a saddled brown gelding. "Gordon says you're welcome to use this horse as long as you need him. He's also loanin' you his 'lucky rope'."

"Thanks."

"Well, hot shot, get mounted. I want to see if you really do know how to rope."

Buck swung up on the gelding and followed Tom to where they would wait their turn to enter the roping boxes. Their attention was drawn to the front of the chutes as one of the ropers tried to get his horse to go into the box. The horse balked and spun. The rider hooked it in the shoulder with his spur and made the horse spin until it seemed it would fall. Then he took his coiled rope and began hitting the horse over the head. The horse ducked and snorted, terrified and confused.

Tom sighed in disgust. "Now that's what I call a real effective trainin' method."

"Who is that?" Buck couldn't believe anyone would do that to a horse, especially in front of the other ropers.

"Eric Vance. As you can see, he's a real swell fella. He's probably higher than a kite. It makes me sick. The Creator never intended for a man to treat an animal that way."

Buck looked intently at Tom. He'd felt drawn to the roper from the first time he'd seen him, and now he sensed the full force of the man's spirit. "Shouldn't we stop him before he ruins that horse?"

Tom shook his head. "As sickening as it is, it's best not to get between a man and his horse unless the situation is totally out of control. Besides, I have a feelin' that horse is already ruined. Crossin' Vance would only cause him to take it out even more on the horse later."

"Yes, but . . ."Buck never got a chance to finish. Vance finally got his horse in the box and made his run. Now it was their turn to rope. They rode to the box and backed their horses into position against the rail.

Tom checked with Buck. "Are you ready?"

"All set." It felt good to be roping again.

Tom nodded for the steer. The chute gate opened, and the steer charged out into the arena. The gray was on it in a couple of strides. Tom threw a fast loop that settled neatly around the steer's horns. He jerked his slack, set the steer and turned off. Buck's horse positioned them so they were right on the corner when Tom slowed the steer and turned back down the arena with it. Buck threw his loop and caught both hind legs of the steer as they come off the ground. He dallied his rope around the saddle horn before the brown gelding stopped hard and the two ropes came tight. Tom turned his horse to face Buck. It was a perfect run. The other ropers were hooting and hollering their approval. Buck and Tom followed their steer to the holding pen at the other end of the arena. They removed their ropes and rode back to the group of riders. Several ropers congratulated them on their run.

"Not bad, kid. Not bad at all."

Buck turned in the saddle to see Eric Vance riding up beside him. Eric's horse was dripping with sweat and breathing hard, but its rider looked cool and confident. "Say, how'd you like to rope heels for me?"

Before he could answer, Tom moved his horse beside Buck's. "Sorry Vance, but I'm invitin' him to be my full-time partner. If you'll remember, my other partner got married and left the valley. Buck will rope with me."

Eric Vance's black eyes danced with the light of steel daggers. "Who says? Let the kid speak for himself. Well, kid . . .?"

Buck studied Vance for a moment. The man's black hair, black eyes, dark complexion and flashy smile made him an attractive man, but there was something weak about him. He was too smooth, too clean. "I'm sorry, but I'm ropin' with Tom."

Vance tried to shrug off Buck's rejection. "That's okay. I just thought I'd ask. I don't' need you anyway. And you're right. You'll be sorry." With that, he reined his horse roughly around and rode away.

Tom shrugged as he watched Vance leave. "Don't worry about it. He's always shootin' off his mouth. He has a hot air problem."

Buck grinned in mutual understanding. He had a feeling he was going to get along with Tom like a brother.

♦♦♦

After the late evening roping, Ben had gotten Ellie up early the next morning for haying. The weather held, and Ben kept cutting the fields. They'd been haying ever since, and Ellie was exhausted. Her body ached everywhere. She was getting her wish. Every day of the past week she'd gone out to the field to help stack hay, determined to hold up her end of the job. At first, the men tried to spare her. She felt like more of a burden than a help. But, after a while, they began to admire her persistence, and they let her get her full share of work. Now, Ellie wasn't so sure her persistence was paying off. However, there were some advantages to this haying business. She didn't have to cook because she and Ben were eating all their meals in the cook shack. Ellie couldn't imagine haying and having to cook, too. Although, Ben told her many ranch wives did just that. If that was the case, Ellie wasn't sure being a ranch wife was such a hot idea.

Physically, she benefited, too. She was becoming stronger and getting in better shape. Ellie loved being out of the house and in the open air. She smiled as she remembered her first attempt to stack hay. The bales seemed to drag her around instead of her being able to put them where she wanted them. One time, she almost fell off the stack trying to keep an unruly bale from going over the edge. It had given her a scare, and she learned there were times when it was best to let go. But now, she was in control, and even though the bales were heavy, she could handle them with confidence.

There was one drawback, though. She was too tired at night for her riding lessons with Buck. However, she didn't want to forget what she learned, so she had the cook help her occasionally, but she missed being with Buck. She hadn't talked to him for a week. He was always out riding somewhere. When she did see him in the cook shack, there was never a chance to talk to him. Ellie wasn't about to tip her hand by going over to sit with him.

Saturday finally brought her the relief she was looking for. More hay was down and curing, but none was ready to be picked up. Ben had gone to town to get parts for the machinery, leaving Ellie alone to do whatever she liked. She decided to practice what she'd learned about riding.

The beautiful day was cool with a slight breeze. Ellie put on her boots and headed for the barn. She got a halter from the tack room and went out to the holding corral. The buckskin gelding stood head-to-tail with another horse, lazily swishing flies and dozing in the warm sun. Ellie opened the gate and stepped into the corral. All heads momentarily raised to see if any food was coming. When none was offered, dozing resumed.

"Hi, fella. Remember me?" Ellie approached the gelding, smiling as she thought about the impression she must have made on the horse.

The gelding didn't appear to see Ellie coming, but when she went to put the lead rope around his neck, he sidled a few steps out of her reach.

"Come on now, I won't hurt you. Be a good boy and let me catch you."

The gelding was unimpressed. He continued his game of cat and mouse. Ellie was beginning to get hot, in more ways than one. Patience was not one of her virtues.

"Would you stand still, please?" She looked grimly at the horse. It was humiliating to think she'd been reduced to talking to a horse. Again the gelding stepped out of Ellie's reach.

"I quit. No horse is worth this. You can stay here and rot for all I care." She turned to leave the corral.

"Don't quit now. You were just about to have him beggin' for mercy."

Ellie jumped at the sound of the voice. "Buck! Where did you come from?"

"I work here, remember?"

Ellie blushed. "Buck, why can't I catch this horse? You said he was gentle." Her voice accused him.

"He is gentle, but he's also smart. He's been around a while. He knows people carryin' halters means work, and he doesn't want to work unless he has to. You're going to have to convince him you're boss."

"How do I do that?"

"By your attitude. You have to walk in that corral knowin' you're going to catch that horse, not just hopin' you are. Once you set out to catch a horse, never quit until you've caught him, even if it takes all day. Now go in there and catch your horse."

"But I . . ."

"Just do it. I'll be in the barn. Call me when you've caught him, and we'll go for a ride."

Ellie sighed. What a fun way to spend a Saturday! With her luck, they'd probably end up going on a moonlight ride. She turned back to the buckskin and started toward him determined to win.

One hour later, a tired, but triumphant Ellie led the buckskin into the barn. Buck looked up from his work. "I was about to give up on you. I'm glad to see you two came to an understandin'."

Ellie wasn't sure she and the horse had come to an "understandin'." It was more like a compromise.

"Buck, I've one question. How can we go riding when I still don't know how to ride very well?"

Buck flashed her a charming smile. "You can practice on the way."

Ellie mumbled something inaudible under her breath, as Buck walked out the door to get his horse. She should've known it would be like this. She would just have to make the best of it and hope she didn't make a fool out of herself.

Buck came back with his horse and tied it to the hitching rail. He went to the tack room for his saddle. Even though she'd been successful a few times, Ellie still watched closely and tried to imitate his every move. She wasn't expecting any sympathy and was thankful for the exercise she'd had haying when it came time to lift the saddle on her horse. As always, it felt like it weighed a ton.

"Are you ready?"

Ellie didn't feel ready, but there was no point in postponing the inevitable. "I guess so."

"Well, mount up, and let's go. And don't forget to check your cinch."

He must be going soft, Ellie thought. She had forgotten about checking her cinch to make sure it was tight enough to keep the saddle from rolling, but not so tight that it interfered with the horse's breathing. Maybe Buck cared about what happened to her after all. She figured he would've enjoyed a good laugh seeing her hanging up-side-down under her horse's belly.

This time, Ellie mounted her horse without looking like a trick rider doing a suicide drag. She noticed Buck stayed on the ground until she was safely in the saddle, then he mounted up. He winced and groaned as he settled himself on his horse.

Ellie was curious. "What happened to you?"

"I've been working with the blue roan."

"Dare I ask who's winning?"

Buck sighed. "I'm afraid she is. I'm going to have to come up with a different approach to my training before she wears me out. The other colts are coming along fine, but she's a tough one. There's got to be a way to get through to her."

Ellie grinned impishly. "Maybe if you gave her a sweet name, she'd live up to it. I think you should name her Kitty."

Buck shot her a doubtful look. "I think Diablo would be more fitting."

Ellie shook her head. "No way. I'm naming her Kitty!"

Buck, resigned, turned his horse towards the distant mountains. "I hope your plan works. Kitty it is."

As they rode, Ellie began to relax and become more a part of her horse. She loved the pungent smell of hot pine needles along the trail that wound its way through the Ponderosas. She also enjoyed watching Buck when he wasn't looking. He moved as one with his horse. It gave her a strange aching feeling in her chest.

As they rode along, Buck gave her helpful pointers. By the time they returned to the ranch, she was feeling right at home on her horse, but when they got to the barn, they both dismounted a little stiffly.

Buck turned to Ellie. "You'll feel the soreness worse tomorrow. It'll take you about a week of ridin' to get your muscles used to it."

Ellie groaned. "Thanks for the encouraging words."

"Don't mention it. By the way, are you doin' anything tomorrow afternoon?"

"No, I don't think so. Why?"

"There's a jackpot team ropin' at Gordon's. I was wonderin' if you'd like to go along."

Ellie looked long and hard at Buck. Was this just a friendly invitation or was there something more? She had to have time to think, so she stalled. "What's a jackpot?"

"In a jackpot, every man pays an entry fee. The more men, the bigger the pot. When the ropin' is over, the winnin' teams split the pot on a percentage, dependin' on the number of teams entered. Well, are you going to go?"

"Sure, I might as well. I've nothing better to do." Ellie was thrilled at the idea of going with Buck, but she wasn't about to let him know it.

"I'll pick you up around twelve-thirty."

♦♦♦

Buck and Ellie arrived at Gordon's with time to spare. Buck caught the horse Gordon loaned him. He tied him to his trailer and got his saddle out of the tack compartment and saddled him. He spoke to Ellie while getting his rope out of his rope can. "Make yourself at home. I'm going out with Gordon to bring in the steers."

"Okay."

The afternoon temperature was in the low nineties, so Ellie found a big tree and sat down in the shade. Vague thoughts played through her mind until she began to doze.

"Well, hello, pretty lady."

Ellie woke with a start. She struggled to focus her eyes on the man standing over her. His face was dark. He grinned, revealing a picture perfect set of teeth. It was Eric Vance. Ellie was simultaneously frightened and thrilled. The man was attractive in a dangerous way; Ellie liked flirting with danger. "I don't believe we've been introduced."

"I'm Eric Vance. Who might you be, and where have you been hiding?"

"My name is Ellie. I'm working for my uncle, Ben Magruder, for the summer. And I haven't been hiding."

Eric's eyes narrowed, sizing Ellie up. "Did you come with somebody?"

Ellie had played this game before, and she knew she could win. "I came with Buck Eagle Plume. He works for Ben, too."

The charming smile never left Vance's face. "How convenient. He's a nice enough kid, but you're kind of out of his class, aren't you?"

Ellie didn't like the way the conversation was going. She wanted to defend Buck, but she knew that's what Vance was fishing for. She changed the subject. "By the way, where's your friend?"

"You mean Morgan? I let her off her leash for a while so she could enjoy the scenery."

That did it! This guy came across as a first class creep. Ellie decided to nip his advances in the bud, so she got up to walk away. "I have to go find Buck."

Eric stepped in front of her and blocked her departure. "Say now, don't be in such a hurry to leave. We're just getting to know each other. By now Morgan has probably sniffed out your friend Buck, and I'm sure she'll keep him entertained in your absence."

Ben and Gordon's words came rushing back to Ellie. The thought of Morgan Knight being with Buck made her sick. She could feel the anger welling up inside of her. Had Eric been watching more closely, he would've seen the green eyes turning black. "Get out of my way . . . now!"

"And if I don't . . . ?"

♦♦♦

It took Buck and Gordon longer than usual to bring in the steers. They were in the brush, fighting flies, and were not about to leave their sanctuary. Gordon had to send his dog into the brush to bring them out. It was hard work, but the dog was good at his job of herding and soon had the steers heading for the corrals. Gordon took off his hat and wiped his brow.

"You can't beat a good dog in brush. He saves me a lot of legwork." The remark was punctuated by a stream of tobacco juice expertly aimed at a rock on the ground.

Buck grinned. Gordon was about as pure old time cowboy as one could get. "How long have you been ranchin', Gordon?"

"As far back as I can remember, and some beyond that. I did take time out to be a deputy sheriff for a while, but ranchin's what I know best."

Buck and Gordon rode the rest of the way to the corrals in silence, enjoying the day and looking forward to the competition. They turned the steers over to the other ropers when they reached the corrals. Buck took his horse for a short drink of water, loosened the cinch and tied him to the arena fence. He needed to pay his entry fee, so he found the secretary's table and stood in line waiting to pay.

"Say, sugar, you look kind of lonesome. "A willowy blond walked up and slipped her arm through his. "A handsome hunk like you shouldn't be standing here all alone."

Buck stared, surprised by the woman's bold approach. Her face was framed with abundant, wavy golden hair, and a small, pouting mouth complimented her thin, straight, slightly upturned nose. Her eyes were large, wide set and ice blue.

Buck and the Blue Roan

Buck gathered his wits and spoke. "Do I know you?"

"No sugar, you don't, but the possibilities are endless." She moved closer to him.

Buck resented the woman's insinuation. He stepped away from her. "Excuse me, but I've business to take care of."

"Anything you say, sugar. Maybe later." With that, the blond turned and walked away.

Buck finished writing his check and was heading back to his horse when he heard a man and woman arguing under the near-by trees. He shook his head in disgust. It bothered him that couples felt free to air their differences in public. Then something about the woman's voice made him look in their direction. It was hard for Buck to see who it was because the woman had her back to him, but the auburn hair could belong to only one person—Ellie, and the man she was talking to was Eric Vance.

Buck didn't wait to see how the conversation would go. In a few strides, he reached the tree. "Ellie, are you all right?"

Relief flooded Ellie's face. "I will be as soon as Mr. Vance gets out of my face."

Buck turned on Eric. "It appears the lady's tired of your company. I would suggest you stay away from her!"

Eric stepped threateningly toward Buck. "Why should I? I don't see your brand on her?"

"That's your trouble, Vance. You think you can treat people the way you treat your horses, and I've seen how you treat your horses. I don't ever want you botherin' Ellie again."

"You think you can back that up, kid?"

Buck's eyes held Eric's in a steady gaze. Dangerous lights danced in the brown depths. "I guess there's a way for you to find out."

"Hey, Buck, where've you been? I've been looking all over for you. "Tom was leading his horse in their direction. He grinned broadly, apparently unaware of the tension that surrounded the little group under the tree.

Vance glared at Buck. "There'll be another time. You can count on it."

Hell Hath No Fury

"ARE YOU ALL RIGHT?" Buck sensed Ellie's agitation and touched her arm.

"I'll be okay in a few minutes. Thanks for coming when you did. That guy is a real creep. I thought he'd leave me alone when I called his bluff, but he didn't give up. I guess Uncle Ben and Gordon were right about him."

Her comment sparked Buck's curiosity. "What did they tell you?"

"They told me Eric and Morgan are bad news. People around here think they're involved in stealing cattle, but nobody's been able to prove it."

"Excuse me, but I don't believe I've had the pleasure." Tom, wanting to bring Buck out of his dangerous mood, flashed a dashing smile at Ellie and tipped his hat.

Buck had been so interested in Eric he'd forgotten his partner was standing there. "This is Ellie Parker, Ben Magruder's niece. And, Ellie, this is Tom Ford, my new ropin' partner."

Tom looked at Ellie with open admiration. "Pleased to make your acquaintance. By the way, Buck, what was going on here?"

"Ellie and our friend, Mr. Vance, were havin' a small disagreement. I told him to move on."

"Oh, he must've really liked that. I bet he wants to be your best buddy now."

"Not likely. I don't think we'll have to worry about him anymore. Now, let's go do what we came here to do—win this ropin'." Buck took Ellie's hand and walked back to his horse. She made no attempt to pull her hand away from him. She glanced back at Tom and noticed a dark cloud of concern shadowing his face.

◆◆◆

Buck's prediction came true. He and Tom won the roping. They soon became the hottest team in the valley. They practiced twice a week at Gordon's and competed at jackpots and rodeos on the weekends.

Their friendship deepened. The older man had a calm wisdom and a strong sense of who he was that gave Buck something solid to lean on. Many evenings they talked long into the night about Native American issues, rodeo and Buck's future. Buck shared his doubts and questions with Tom openly. It was good for him to get his feelings out where he could deal with them. On one such evening, Buck tried to explain to Tom the trouble he was having with his grandfather. "Tom, I'm worried. I can't get through to my grandfather, and it scares me. He and Rusty are the only close family I have, and I don't like the anger that's come between us. Every time I try to get him to tell me what he's feeling, he pulls away. Sometimes it frustrates me so much I say things I shouldn't."

Tom was quiet for a moment, thinking. Finally, he spoke, moving slowly with his words like a man groping his way in the dark. "I don't know anything about being a parent or grandparent, but I do know what it's like coming home from war and trying to get a grip on life again. The Medical Corps was about the worst place to be. Everybody came back from Nam with some dark corners they can't bear to look into, let alone share with their families. You need to cut your grandpa some slack."

Buck squirmed, not liking the direction the conversation was taking. He looked at the ground and concentrated on the little ditch he was digging with the toe of his boot. "I think he uses Vietnam as an excuse."

Tom looked long and hard at Buck. "How's that?"

Buck's emotions welled up inside him like a flooding river behind a dam. He tried to keep himself in check, but the dam was too old and cracked. All of his years of anger, pain and resentment broke through his defenses as the flood of his emotions washed over him and spilled out.

"Damn war! Dad didn't have to go. He joined the Marines. He left Mom alone, knowing she was an alcoholic and pregnant. My brother's handicapped with Fetal Alcohol Syndrome because he left when my mom needed him the most. And you know what's worse? When he did come back, he went to work at the Vet Hospital in Missoula and left me home alone with Mom and Rusty. You know what my strongest childhood memories are? It's the smell of alcohol vomit, the sound of my brother always crying and the loneliness. When we needed Grandfather, he was never around. He was off in the mountains trying to 'find himself.'"

Tom sat silent for a long time before he spoke. "It appears you're packin' a mighty heavy load, kid. I'll help you bear the weight of it, but you're going to have to go to your granddad and get it off your back."

Buck fought back tears as he spoke. "Then I guess I'll have to get used to packin' it because I'm not going to let him off that easy."

Tom got up from his chair on the bunkhouse porch and put on his jean jacket. "I can't tell you what to do, but if you don't get rid of this thing, it will destroy you and your family. A little forgiveness goes a long way. Think about how bad your granddad's hurtin' and why. You two may have more in common than you think."

After Tom had left, Buck crawled into his bunk and lay thinking about his partner's words long into the night. How could he forgive his grandfather for abandoning him? He missed his parents, especially his mom. He tried to find a happy place in his memory where he could see her as she was when things weren't so bad. An image floated softly up from the depths, the image of a fair face, blue eyes and the sun shimmering on her blond hair as she leaned down to pick up a baby chick. He saw her smile as she reached out her hands to him so he could touch the little bit of fluff, and then she was gone. The darkness drew down around him, and the chorus of snoring men went unnoticed.

♦♦♦

Ellie, upset by Eric Vance's effect on her, scolded herself for even giving him a second thought. She'd seen his type in the clubs in Chicago, and his attitude repulsed her, but still he excited her. He was so good looking and sure of himself. Ellie also worried about the implied threats that had passed between him and Buck. The memory of Buck coming to her defense made her heart beat a little faster, and she felt silly for it. Her girlfriends at Oak Park High would call her a traitor to the cause of liberated women everywhere if they knew what she was thinking. She became preoccupied with memories of the incident, but she was too embarrassed to tell Ben what had happened, especially after he'd warned her about Eric.

Ben noticed the change in her behavior. One day at breakfast he spoke to her about it. "Is somethin' botherin' you, Ellie?"

"It's nothing, Uncle Ben. I'm just a little tired, I guess."

"Well, why don't you take the day off and go ridin' with Buck. He's takin' salt to the cattle on the Forest Service lease land. It might do you good to take a break from the work around here."

"Thanks. That would be dope."

Ben looked at her and shrugged. "Kids!"

Later, Ellie finished her chores and went to the corral to catch her horse. She was getting better handling him, and she was even beginning to like the old gelding. After saddling her horse, Ellie went to find Buck. She heard a commotion in the round corral and went to see what was going on. Buck stood in the middle of the corral. He had a long line on the blue roan mare. She bucked violently around him in a circle. The mare wore a pack saddle, and she was desperately trying to unload the panniers full of salt Buck had tied securely to her back. Each pannier contained two fifty pound blocks of salt. The two hundred pounds of dead weight began to tell on the mare. With each turn she made around Buck, her jumps became less and less violent. Finally, she settled into a run, then a trot and then she stopped to face him. She was breathing hard, and some of the fire seemed to have left her eyes.

When all was quiet, Ellie walked over to the fence. "Hey, so Uncle Ben gave me the day off. Mind if I join you on your ride?"

By now Buck cradled the blue roan's head in his arms, rubbing her gently between the eyes. "Not at all. In fact, I welcome the company. It's going to be a long day in the saddle."

Ellie looked at the mare with admiration. The horse was a beautiful animal with her gun-metal blue coat glistening in the sun. "If I didn't know better, I'd say she was as gentle as a kitten. What've you been doing with her?"

"If you watch a horse's eyes you can measure the pressure inside her. Once the white rims no longer show, it's safe to approach her. Ever since I decided to quit fightin' her and let her fight herself, we've been doing better. It's a whole lot easier on me, too. Today she's going to be my pack horse. She can buck all she wants. By the time we get home she should be ready to let me ride her."

"I know you think she's special, but I don't see how you can keep working with her. I would've given up a long time ago."

"Well, mount up and let's get going. I'll see if I can explain it to you on the way."

Buck and Ellie rode north from the main ranch corrals. The two-track road they followed turned into a single stock trail as they left the lower pastures and headed up into the hills. The day promised to heat up as the glaring sun sucked the color from the sky. Ellie was glad for the canteen hanging from her saddle horn, and she hoped the lunch she'd packed didn't get squashed in her saddle bags.

As they rode along, Buck shared his thoughts with her about why he kept working with the blue roan mare. "It's kind of a spiritual thing, I guess. The mare is wild; she has the heart of a grizzly and the spirit of an eagle. There's a part of me that connects with that in her. I respect her. In a way, she has become my Spirit Helper."

Ellie frowned. "Your what?"

"Natives believe that the Great Spirit sends us a special animal to teach us life lessons and to guide and protect us."

Ellie listened without making any comment. She felt unsure of herself when Buck started talking about spiritual things. She'd never given much thought to whether or not a spirit world even existed outside a bottle or a can, let alone thinking of it as a personal reality the way Buck did.

They reached the first salt ground. Buck stopped to unload one of the blocks of salt. He removed one from the other pannier and tied it to the middle of the pack to even the load. The blue mare stood quietly. She was sweating, not from nervous excitement, but from honest work. Buck patted her on the neck. "This ought to take some of the vinegar out of you."

The morning wore on. They left the lower hills and headed into the trees and rougher going. Ellie welcomed the shade. She was hot and beginning to ache in her knees and butt. However, she was not about to complain to Buck. He was ahead of her on the trail. As if he could read her thoughts, he stopped his horse and turned to her. "You might want to get off and walk a spell. It keeps you from stiffenin' up, and it gives your horse a break. We've a lot of ridin' yet to do today."

Ellie was grateful for the chance to get off her horse. She almost collapsed as her feet hit the ground. She hung onto the saddle horn for support. "Are we going to eat lunch pretty soon?"

Buck smiled wryly. "We'll stop in a bit. I know a nice place up the trail. It's along the creek. There's shade for us and grass for the horses."

Ellie walked up the trail after Buck. She inhaled the pungent smell of the hot pine needles coming from the forest floor. It was the most wonderful aroma she'd ever smelled. Ellie was so busy enjoying the forest she didn't notice Buck had stopped. She came dangerously close to colliding with the back end of the blue mare.

"We'll eat lunch here." Buck took the horses across the narrow stream to a grassy glade. He loosened their cinches and pulled their bridles. He then hobbled them to prevent them from heading home. When Buck returned to where Ellie was setting out the lunch in the shade of a huge pine tree, he whistled his appreciation. "Between you and the cook, we're going to have a real feast.

Ellie flushed, embarrassed. "I wasn't sure you'd have a lunch with you."

Buck sat down. "Hey, I'm not complainin'."

Both ravenous, they ate without talking, enjoying the forest and the food. Ellie was in the middle of her second sandwich when she began to feel uneasy. She looked up to see Buck watching her. His eyes were incredibly dark and intense. Suddenly, she felt like running. "I better go check on my horse."

Ellie moved to get up, but Buck's hand on her arm stopped her. "He'll be okay. Just take it easy. We're in no hurry."

"But I . . ."

"Ellie, what are you afraid of?"

Ellie's mind began to whirl. She knew the truth. She was afraid of Buck, of how he made her feel. When she was with him, she wasn't in control of her emotions. After what happened with her dad, she'd vowed she'd never let herself care about another man. She had another fear, too. There was this great chasm between her and Buck. She could not accept his concept of a supernatural world. She felt like he was living in the Dark Ages. Why couldn't he be like other guys? She could deal with them hitting on her, but Buck's calm and control was driving her crazy.

Buck's brow furrowed as he explored Ellie's face. "Ellie, what's botherin' you?"

Ellie was frustrated. Buck, you talk so easy about spiritual things, as if it really matters. I don't even know if I believe there is a God, or gods or anything supernatural."

"That's a place to start. Sometimes I'm not sure either, but I've a gut feelin' that tells me it's true. The elders try to pass on the old ways to us, but it's hard. There are so many distractions. Many kids on the Rez are looking for a different way."

Buck held her arm a little longer than needed before he let go. "We best get back to work."

Ellie rode the rest of the day in silence. It was too hot for anything other than idle conversation. Her mind was in turmoil. At times she was mad at Buck, and she told herself she shouldn't like him. On the other hand, she couldn't resist his rugged hotness or the strength of his will. And then there was this thing about a spirit world. It pissed her off. She'd done just fine without all the hokum of religion, and she hadn't seen anything to make her believe there was anything to it. The only spirits she trusted were the ones found in a bottle, and right now she needed to worship at the altar of alcohol. Why did things have to be so complicated?

Buck and the Blue Roan

♦♦♦

The weeks passed quickly. Buck and Tom practiced for hours in preparation for the Fourth of July rodeo. Eric and Morgan were at all the practice sessions, too. Eric made it perfectly clear he and his new roping partner intended to win the team roping.

Occasionally, Ellie went with Buck to the practices, but being around Eric and Morgan was nerve wracking. Between Eric's meaningful glances and Morgan's obvious interest in Buck, she thought she'd go crazy. To avoid the situation, she started making up excuses why she couldn't go.

She also found herself needing to drink more often. She had stashed a six pack of beer she'd stolen from the cook shack cooler in the barn. This day she needed it more than ever. She had her back to the barn doorway and was pushing her hand deep between the hay bales.

Buck came around the corner of the barn, so intent on his purpose he didn't give Ellie's strange behavior much thought. He hoped to break the ice, so he cleared his throat and spoke. "There's a rodeo in Hamilton. Do you want to come?"

Ellie whirled around with a frightened expression on her face. "What the hell! You scared me! What are you doing sneaking up on me like that?"

Buck didn't think he'd been sneaking, but he apologized for scaring her, and then he asked again. "Well, do you want to go or not?"

Ellie struggled to gain her composure. "Sure . . . yeah, I'll go. I've been wanting to go to a rodeo for ages. Well, I guess I better get up to the house and start fixing supper for Uncle Ben."

Ellie brushed past Buck and hurried up the path to the ranch house. As she passed him, Buck caught a faint smell of beer. Immediately he felt the effect; his stomach knotted, and a wave of sick heat washed over him. He watched Ellie enter the house, and then he turned to the haystack. Part of him wanted to walk away; part of him had to know. Slowly he pushed his hand between the bales until his fingers touched the cool silkiness of aluminum. He grabbed the can and pulled it out. The sunlight behind him glared off the familiar label, mocking him with its brightness. He hurled the can against the barn wall and watch in cold anger as it sprayed its contents into the dust of the barnyard.

Buck and Ellie left the ranch early enough to give him plenty of time to pay his entry fees and warm up his horse before the rodeo. The ride to the fairgrounds passed in awkward silence. Buck wasn't good at fishing for answers, but he didn't think he should come right out and ask Ellie if she was drinking. So after they talked about the weather, how the haying was going and the horses, their conversation died. When they got to Hamilton, Buck pulled into the fairgrounds and parked his rig. "You can stay here if you like, or you can get a seat in the grandstands. The view and the shade are better up there."

"Thanks. I think I'll get a grandstand seat. I don't want to miss any of the action. It'll be fun watching you and Tom win the team roping. Without looking at him, Ellie got out of the truck and headed for the ticket office. She never looked back.

Puzzled, Buck watched her go. As long as he lived, he figured he would never understand women, but it made him feel good to know she was rooting for him. He spoke to her receding back. "Thanks . . . I think."

"Hi, sugar. I thought your girlfriend would never leave." Morgan opened the passenger's door and slipped in beside Buck. Unnerved by her sudden appearance, he couldn't reply.

Morgan moved closer to Buck and slid her arm knowingly through his. "It's a long time until the rodeo starts. Why don't we go someplace where we can get to know each other better?" She leaned in and tried to kiss him.

Buck's body reacted before his mind did. Disgusted, he pushed her away. "You just don't get the picture, do you, Morgan? You're not my type."

Morgan's voice held a dangerous edge. "I suppose little Miss Chicago's your type. Well, after Eric gets through with her, you won't want her."

Buck's eyes narrowed. "What's that supposed to mean?"

"Figure it out for yourself. Or didn't your mama tell you about the birds and the bees?" Morgan slid across the seat and out the door. She gave Buck a deadly look, then slammed the door shut. "You're going to be real sorry you turned me down . . . Half-breed."

Missing Saddles

ELLIE SHOWED HER TICKET to the man at the gate and was then caught up in the flow of people pouring in toward the grandstands. The crowd was a mix of locals and tourists, and it was easy to tell which was which. Old men in baggy, faded jeans had come to kindle memories of better times. They were accompanied by their wives, who were patiently tolerant of old men and their memories. Young couples arrived, towing dirty-faced children. They were too busy with their families to realize they were making their own memories. And there were teenagers filled with too many dreams to worry about memories. Most of them hadn't come to see the rodeo. For them, it was all about the social rituals of adolescence.

Finally, there were the tourists. Ellie smiled at what she saw, but she didn't laugh. She knew she would've looked like they did if she hadn't been living in Montana for a while. The people she saw were either overdressed or barely dressed. The over-dressed people were marked by their new boots, hats, shirts and jeans. They were the obvious dudes. The under-dressed tourists were mainly women sporting dark sunglasses, halter tops and short shorts. Many of them were white skinned and overweight. Ellie was embarrassed for them and a bit sorry, too. There would be many painful sunburns before the day was over.

Ellie worked her way up through the stands until she found a place where she had a good view of the arena. She put her purse beside her to save a spot for Ben when he came, and she then settled down to enjoy the rodeo.

The arena filled with men and women who were riding their horses to warm them up. The rodeo announcer tested the P.A. system as he called for various people to report to the rodeo office to check in for their event. Ellie searched the area, anxious to catch sight of Buck and Tom.

She felt a knot of excitement tighten in her stomach as she thought of these two men. Buck and Tom really were a team. Tom, outgoing and funny, was becoming like the big brother she never had. She could see he was good for Buck, and she was thankful for their growing friendship. Buck, on the other hand, remained quiet and intense. He only said what was necessary: nothing more. His humor was subtler than Tom's, but it was just as effective. Both Buck and Tom could make her laugh and just being with them made her feel more alive. Ellie knew she would have a hard time being satisfied now by her friends in Chicago.

Chicago . . . she hadn't thought about going back until this moment. The awful realization came to her that she wasn't looking forward to returning. The sales at Marshall Fields or knowing how the Bears were doing this season no longer seemed important. She had grown to love Montana and the people who lived here. This revelation disturbed her. She hadn't meant to form any emotional attachments; she didn't need them nor want them; yet, now she knew she wanted to stay. Going back would only make her life worse than before. Before she drank because she was bored; now she knew she would drink to forget.

"Have I missed anything?" Ben picked up Ellie's purse and handed it to her as he sat down beside her.

Ellie looked up, startled out of her reverie. "Oh, hi, Uncle Ben. No, the rodeo hasn't started."

"You seemed kind of far away. Did I interrupt a good dream?" Ben grinned.

Ellie felt the heat rising in her cheeks. "No, I was just thinking about Chicago."

"Do you miss it?" Ben's expression changed from cheerful teasing to one of worry.

"No, I don't. That's the problem. I don't think I want to go back; not to spend the rest of my life there, anyway."

"Is there any reason you have to go back? You can stay with me as long as you like, you know." Ben put his arm around Ellie's shoulder and gave her an affectionate squeeze.

"Uncle Ben, I can't do that. I can't take advantage of your hospitality. Besides, I have to go back to find a way to earn my high school diploma, since I got kicked out of school."

"Who's takin' advantage? You're earnin' your keep, and if you need to go to school, we can probably find something in Missoula."

"But how would it look to Buck? He'd think I was staying here just to chase after him." Ellie faked a cough and looked quickly away. She hadn't meant to think that, let alone say it out loud.

Ben maintained an innocent expression with difficulty. "What does Buck have to do with it? He'll be done with the colts in a few months, and then he'll be headin' back to the Flathead. You don't have to ever see him again if you don't want to."

Ellie's throat tightened. "I forgot he'd be leaving."

Ben couldn't resist teasing her. "Don't tell me you've been stayin' on with me just on account of him."

Ellie's face flushed. "Uncle Ben, that's so bogus. I love you, and I love the ranch and . . . I'm really thirsty. I think I'll go get a cold drink. Would you like something?"

Ellie didn't wait for Ben's reply. She got up and wormed her way through the crowd to the steps down from the stands.

Ben watched Ellie go, a mixed expression of awe and love on his face. He hadn't realized until this moment how important it was to have family near. Her leaving would only make the loneliness lonelier. He called after her. "Get me a lemonade . . . please."

♦♦♦

Buck sat in the pickup thinking about Morgan and her implied threat. Both she and Eric were like a couple of characters out of a bad movie. He felt a little sorry for Morgan, though. He wondered how someone that young could be so used up. Buck was more worried about Ellie. He could handle Morgan, but could Ellie handle Eric? Morgan's insinuation bothered him. He'd have to tell Ellie to stay clear of Eric. However, for the time being, she was safe. Eric would be too busy getting ready for the team roping to worry about causing trouble for her. After he sorted the events of the past few weeks, Buck shook his head in disgust and got out of the truck to unload his horse. His life was beginning to get too complicated. All he wanted was to be left alone so he could rodeo the way he wanted. He saddled up and left his horse tied to the trailer, while he went to pay his entry fee and pick up his contestant number.

Tom was already waiting in line at the rodeo office. "Hi, Buck. Say, are you feelin' okay? You look a little drawn up in the flanks."

Buck grinned. Tom sure had a funny way of putting things. "I'm fine. I just had a little misunderstandin' with Morgan Knight a few minutes ago."

Tom had a knowing look on his face. "Tell me, what's that sweet young thing up to now?"

Buck's face reddened. "Trouble as usual. She tried to put the moves on me, but I turned her down. She doesn't take rejection kindly."

Tom chuckled. "I don't imagine she does."

"She made a few threats about how I would be sorry, and that Eric would take care of Ellie. What she said about Ellie worries me. I think Vance is capable of doing anything."

"Don't worry. I have a feelin' Ellie can take care of herself, but it won't hurt to keep our eyes and ears open. By the way, where is she?"

"She should be up in the grandstands with Ben." Buck shielded his hat brim with his hand to cut down the sun's glare, but he could not find Ellie and Ben in the growing crowd.

Buck and Tom paid their fees and then took their horses to the arena to warm them up. As they rode, Buck searched the stands again for a glimpse of Ellie. Tom watched with interest, his eyes twinkling with mischief. "She's about the best-lookin' gal I've ever seen."

"Who?"

"Ellie."

Buck's face heated up. "She may be pretty, but sometimes she acts like a spoiled kid, and . . ."

"Now, Buck, if you were as good lookin' as she is, you'd be a little spoiled, too. Course you don't ever have to worry about havin' that problem. Tom grabbed his saddle horn as Buck gave him a playful shove.

The announcer's voice blared over the speakers. "Let's clear the arena. Grand entry time will be in five minutes."

Buck patted his horse on the neck. "Let's sit this one out. It's nothing more than a controlled stampede, and I don't need that kind of excitement now."

Buck and Tom returned to the trailer to tie up their horses. They loosened the cinches, so the horses could relax and went back to the arena to find a good spot to watch the action. They had quite a while to wait before it would be time for the team roping.

Soon, dust rose above the arena as the contestants raced in for the grand entry. A hush fell over the crowd as a young girl stepped up to the microphone to sing a squeaky version of the Star Spangled Banner.

While all eyes were turned to the American flag, a shadowy figure slipped between the parked horse trailers and stopped next to Tom's gray gelding. The sun gleamed momentarily on the blade of a sharp knife as a swift hand sawed back and forth on the leather billet strap holding the front cinch of Tom's saddle, cutting it almost completely through.

♦♦♦

Ellie returned with two cold drinks, feeling silly for having left in such a rush. She wished she didn't get so rattled every time she thought about Buck. What made it worse was she knew Ben knew how she felt. Her humiliation was complete.

Ben smiled up at her. "Glad to see you made it back. I was beginning to think you ran off with one of those cowboys."

Ellie handed Ben his cup. "There was a long line at the refreshment stand. I hope you like what I got."

"Since the waitress ran off before I could put in my order, I have no choice." Ben grinned at Ellie and gave her hand an affectionate squeeze.

The rodeo was underway. Ellie's attention was riveted on the arena. She clutched Ben's arm during the bronc riding, sure that both the horse and the rider were going to be killed. Sometimes she cheered for the horses, and sometimes she cheered for the riders. She hated the calf roping. It seemed like such a cruel thing to do to a baby animal. Ben had tried to explain to her earlier that it was an art the cowboys were trying to keep alive, and it was very difficult to catch one of those little calves. Still, she closed her eyes and prayed the cowboys would miss their catch. The barrel racing, however, thrilled her. How anybody could stay on a horse going that fast boggled her mind. She appreciated the horsemanship of these women riders, especially after her own limited experience staying on a horse.

Finally, the announcer called for the team ropers. Ellie's grip tightened on Ben's arm. "I hope Buck and Tom win."

Ben chuckled. "I hope my arm makes it through this rodeo."

Ellie gave his arm a softer squeeze and then let go. "I'm sorry, Uncle Ben, but this is so exciting I'm getting stressed."

The roping teams milled around outside the entrance to the arena while they waited for their turn to rope. Eric Vance and his partner were the third team up. Buck and Tom drew the last position.

The first two teams out had bad luck. On the first team's run, the header missed his throw. During the second team's run, the heeler caught only one back leg, adding a five-second penalty to their time.

Eric rode into the box with confidence. Ellie noticed how good looking he was in his black hat and red and black striped shirt. Once again, she felt attracted to him in spite of what she knew. Eric's run was almost perfect with a time of seven point nine seconds.

Ben whistled softly. "They're going to be hard to beat. I don't like the guy, but I have to admit he's a darn good roper."

"Do you think Buck and Tom can beat them?" Ellie fidgeted nervously on the hard plank seat.

"They can if they don't have any bad luck. We'll just have to wait and see."

The rest of the ropers seemed to take forever. Ellie wanted to go down and tell them to hurry up. She didn't know how Buck and Tom could sit so quietly, waiting for their turn to rope.

Finally, the announcer called them to the roping box. Ellie wasn't aware she was holding her breath. She watched

Tom back his horse into position, followed by Buck. There was a moment's hesitation while both ropers made sure their horses and the steer were ready to make the run. They wanted the steer to look straight ahead and their horses to be watching the steer. Buck signaled he was ready to go. Tom took one last look at the steer and nodded his head. The chute gate opened with a loud clang, and the steer bolted for freedom.

The powerful gray gelding came out of the roping box like it had been shot from a cannon. In a few strides, it had its rider in position at the steer's hip. Tom made two fast swings of his rope, and then threw his loop. The loop settled neatly around the steer's horns and came tight as Tom jerked his slack. He checked the gray to set the steer, and then he turned off to start logging it away so Buck could rope both of the steer's back legs.

At that moment, what looked like a picture perfect run turned into total chaos. The strain of the horse and the steer pulling against each other tore the partially severed billet strap of Tom's saddle all the way through. Tom felt the saddle start to roll, so he bailed off. The gray started bucking in confusion and fear.

Buck stopped his horse hard to avoid running over the steer and crashing into Tom. He leaped from his horse and ran to Tom, who was on the ground with his arms around his head to protect himself from his horse's flying hooves. The bucking gray leaped over Tom, its back feet barely missing Tom's head as they hit the ground. Buck grabbed his partner and pulled him out of the way of the still frantic horse. With the help of some other ropers, they finally caught Tom's horse and got it calmed down enough to take off what was left of the saddle that was now hanging under its belly.

Tom looked at Buck in despair. "Would you look at that? Of all the rotten luck."

Buck tried to cheer up his partner. "Hey, I know a good saddle maker in Hamilton. He likes a challenge. He'll have your saddle fixed in no time."

"Thanks, Buck, but this saddle's seen its last ride." Tom turned to check his horse for injuries. The horse was snorting and shaking, but it was uninjured.

Buck began picking up pieces of the broken saddle. He found what was left of the billet out where Tom's horse had started bucking. As he turned it over in his hands, the slick edges of the knife cut caught his attention. He whistled softly under his breath. "This explains it."

The bull riding was about to begin, so Buck caught his horse, and then hurried out of the arena and over to Tom's trailer. His partner was throwing what was left of his saddle in the back of his pickup. Buck handed him the severed billet. "Take a look at this."

Tom took the piece of leather and looked at it casually until he saw the knife cut. "Of all the low-down, dirty tricks. I'd like to get my hands on the skunk that did this."

"Sorry about the bad luck, fellas." Gordon Ritter approached the truck.

Tom handed him the severed billet strap. "It had nothin' to do with bad luck."

"What do you mean?" Gordon took the leather strap and turned it over in his hand.

"Take a look at this knife cut. Somebody wanted to make real sure we didn't win the team ropin'."

Gordon swore under his breath. "This looks bad. I was on my way over here to tell you fellas to lock up your saddles. Craig King just had his saddle stolen right off his horse that was tied to his trailer."

Tom slapped his hat against his leg. "That does it! I'm going over to have a little talk with Vance."

Gordon reached out and grabbed Tom's arm. "Now hold on a minute. We don't know for sure who's doing this. If it is Vance, he's too smart to get caught. He won't have any evidence on him. He never does. We'll have to catch him in the act, if we want to prove he's the one stealin' saddles. In the meantime, the best thing for you to do is to stay cool."

Buck could see the struggle going on inside of Tom. He put his hand on his partner's shoulder. "Gordon's right. We'll just have to keep a close eye on Eric. He'll mess up sooner or later."

Tom clenched his jaw. "I hope you're right, but I'd rather clock him right now."

Buck looked grimly at his friend. "I know what you mean."

At that moment, Ben and Ellie came rushing up. Ellie's face was pale. "Buck, are you all right? I was terrified you were going to be killed, and all I could do was sit there and watch. It was awful!"

Tom grinned sardonically. "I'm fine. Thanks, Ellie!"

Ellie's concern filled Buck with a warm feeling of tenderness he had not felt in a very long time. The feeling was embarrassing, so he tried to shrug it off. "I'm okay. Tom was the one who almost lost his head."

Ellie smiled sweetly. "Well, thank heavens you're both okay."

For a moment, Ellie wondered at the men's casual attitude. She decided it must be a guy thing. She was about to say something when she saw Gordon talking to Ben. She moved closer, so she could overhear what they were saying. As Gordon explained to Ben about the missing tack and the sabotage of Tom's saddle, Ellie began to blush with anger. To think she'd been flirting with the idea of hooking up with Eric Vance made her ashamed. If he'd really done these things, he really was a dangerous person. She felt like a traitor. Ellie resolved never to let herself be taken in by Eric's charm and good looks again.

Dumped Again

BUCK VIGOROUSLY BRUSHED the blue mare. Over the summer, the sun had faded the gun-metal blue hair coat to a soft gray-blue. He ran his hand over her sleek coat. As the months passed, the mare had learned to trust Buck, but she would never enjoy human companionship. She would do what she had to do and would be asked to be left alone in return. Buck understood and accepted this. There was a mutual feeling of respect between the two of them.

There was another thing about the mare Buck had learned to accept. She was a compulsive bucker. She no longer bucked out of fear or meanness. It was more an involuntary reaction, like somebody sneezing when their nose was tickled. Buck didn't take it personally when the mare started pitching with him. He knew it was her nature. The only thing that bothered him was the fact that he hadn't learned to stay off her.

Today was going to be the true test of their relationship. He'd been riding her to check on the cattle for several weeks. Now it was time for him to take her to Gordon's ranch and introduce her to the sport of team roping. Buck smiled to himself. He knew the mare would have an opinion of her own about the matter.

The ranch was uncommonly quiet for a Saturday. Ellie had gone to town with Ben for the day. Buck loaded the blue mare in his trailer and headed to Gordon's. As he drove, his thoughts turned to the events of the summer. The young cowboy was satisfied with the progress the three-year-olds were making. Ben had raised a nice bunch of horses. That part of this stay in the Bitterroots gave him satisfaction, but he was disturbed by the trouble with Eric Vance. There had to be a way to catch him if he was the one stealing the saddles.

Another thing bothered him. He found himself thinking about Ellie more than he would like to admit. At first, he thought it was just his concern for her physical safety, but it had gone beyond that now. Buck had to admit to himself that he was strongly attracted to her, and he was having a difficult time coping with the feelings of desire she aroused in him.

Buck knew it was dangerous for him to become emotionally involved with this white girl, especially an alcoholic one at that. Differences in their cultures and beliefs could tear a relationship apart; add alcohol to the mixture, and it would be trouble for sure. He'd already felt the tension with Ellie whenever he talked about his spiritual beliefs. Now he wanted to hold her so bad it made his palms sweat, and his own desire scared him. He knew he should run from this situation because there was too much at stake, but he also felt compelled to stay and confront Ellie about her drinking problem. Maybe if he did, he could keep her from making the same mistakes his mother made.

By the time Buck pulled into Gordon's driveway, Gordon had the roping steers in the corral and ready to go. Gordon waved to him and called out good-naturedly, "I thought maybe you changed your mind in favor of a quieter Saturday mornin' activity. It's a little early for bronc ridin' don't ya think?"

Buck parked his rig and got out. "Hey, now, don't believe all those nasty rumors you've heard about my new horse. She's as gentle as a kitten."

Gordon watched Buck unload the mare. She came flying backward out of the old trailer, head up, and her eyes white-rimmed and looking for trouble. Gordon grinned wryly. "Some kitten!"

Buck patted the mare's sweat-drenched neck. "She's just a little nervous. She'll settle down in a few minutes."

Buck saddled the mare carefully. He tightened the cinch a little at a time, giving the mare a chance to get used to the constricting sensation of the cinch around her girth. When he was satisfied everything was as it should be, he led the mare to the arena. Gordon was there, loping his horse in big circles to warm it up.

The blue mare was alert, but no longer tense. Her eyes had softened. Buck took this as a good sign. He gathered his reins and eased himself into the saddle. For a moment both he and the mare held their breaths, each waiting to see what the other was going to do. Buck sat quietly, rubbing her neck with his hand, letting the mare settle. When he was confident she wasn't going to explode, he asked her to move out. He let the mare take several turns around the arena at a brisk walk. Then he asked her to jog and then to lope. She humped her back and tried to pull the reins from his hands, but Buck kept her head up. After a while, the mare settled down to a steady gait. If she'd been pressured earlier, he was sure she would've started bucking.

Gordon rode up beside Buck. They eased their horses back to a walk.

"I have to hand it to you, Buck. You sure have come a long way with that mare. What's your plan today?"

"I thought I'd spend the mornin' getting her used to the roping box and trailin' a few steers. If she comes along all right, maybe I can throw a couple of loops off of her later this afternoon."

"Sounds good to me. I'll work the chutes for you." Gordon dismounted and led his horse to the fence where he looped the reins over a wire hook. The seasoned rope horse stood quietly in the warm morning sun.

Buck took his time teaching the mare to back into the far rear corner of the roping box. He rode in and asked her to turn slowly around; then he applied gentle pressure with his legs and a steady pull back on the bit to get her to back. At first, she went along with him, but then she began to get mad as he repeated the maneuver. She started grinding and chomping her teeth against the bit and tossing her head.

Gordon chuckled and spit a brown stream of tobacco juice into the dirt. "Your kitten has a bit of a temper."

Buck grinned. "You could say that. Let's give her a steer to chase. Maybe that will take her focus off fightin' me."

Buck positioned the mare in the box and nodded for a steer. Gordon opened the chute, and the steer made a break for freedom. The mare jumped, startled by the banging noise of the chute gate opening and the sudden appearance of the steer. It was halfway down the arena before Buck could get her to leave the roping box. After several more tries, the mare began to take an interest in the steers. She started to anticipate the chute opening, and she got the hang of gathering herself for that first powerful leap out of the box. Buck was pleased with her progress. "Let's call it quits for a while. I think she's earned a break."

Gordon and Buck turned the steers out for feed and water and put the mare in a stall. Gordon turned to Buck. "How about having some lunch?"

"That sounds good to me. This horse training makes me hungry."

Mrs. Ritter had lunch waiting for Gordon and Buck. They ate in silence, appreciating the beef stew and homemade bread. Finally, Buck spoke. "Have you heard anything more about the saddles that were stolen?"

Gordon took a sip of iced tea to wash down his bite of food. "No. Those saddles are pretty hard to trace unless they are custom built or one someone won in competition. Whoever stole them probably sent them out of state. This looks like a professional job. I've heard that more saddles have turned up missin'."

Buck sighed and shook his head. "Do you think Vance is involved?"

Gordon pushed his chair back and took a toothpick out of the container on the kitchen table. "If he is, he isn't in it by himself. Somebody's helpin' him get rid of the evidence real fast."

Buck shook his head. "I'd like to catch him at it just once."

"We all would. We'll just have to keep our eyes open and take extra precautions. Most of those saddles cost over three thousand dollars. Someone's going to make good money off them."

Having no more answers regarding Eric Vance, Gordon and Buck listened to the local noon news before they went back outside. They ran the steers in and saddled their horses. The blue mare seemed calm and relaxed. After a short warm up period, they decided to try roping a few steers. Everything went well. Buck had spent a lot of time getting the mare used to ropes, so she wasn't bothered by them now. The first few steers out of the box, he worked on getting the mare to stop on her haunches after he made his heel catch. Buck let his dallies slip, so the mare wouldn't take the full jerk of the rope coming tight. He didn't want her to get a sore back. Until she learned to handle herself and the steer, he took it easy on her.

Buck was pleased with the mare's progress. She started putting him in good roping position on the corners, and she was learning to round her body to better take the force of a hard stop after the steer's heels were caught. He turned to Gordon. "Let's run one more steer, and then call it a day."

Buck released the chute gate from the back of his horse and then rode hard after the steer. Ben made a smooth horn catch, and Buck was right behind him. Buck moved the mare into position and made his throw the moment the hard running steer's back legs came off the ground. He jerked his slack and started to dally to the saddle horn, only he couldn't find the saddle horn. When he made his catch, the blue mare bogged her head and ducked off to the right. The rope sizzled through Buck's hand before he could let it go. He fought to get control of the mare's head, but her spin to the right unbalanced him. He felt himself going over the mare's front end. The ground came up to meet him, and he landed hard on his shoulder.

Gordon rode up and dismounted. "That was very impressive. Are you okay?"

Buck grinned sheepishly. "I'm fine. My pride's a little bruised, but my hand . . ."

Buck looked down at his hand. The skin on his fingers was torn off in places, and what was left was seared white and smooth by the rope tearing across it. As the air penetrated the exposed flesh, Buck was reminded how painful a severe rope burn could be. He grimaced in pain. "That's what I get for not wearin' my ropin' gloves. You'd think I'd learn by now."

Buck and the Blue Roan

Gordon helped Buck to his feet. "I've got some stuff at the house we can put on it. We'll wrap it, and you should be as good as new in a couple of weeks."

While Gordon went to the house, Buck caught his mare. She was quietly nibbling grass along the fence and didn't bother to move away as Buck came up to her. "Sure, look innocent. I know how you are."

When Gordon returned, he gave Buck cowboy first aid by slathering the burns with a white cream he used on the horses when they got a cut. He then helped Buck unsaddle and load his horse. "I wouldn't do any ropin' for a few weeks if I was you."

Buck grimaced in pain as he climbed into his truck. "I don't plan on it. Thanks for your help. I'll be back as soon as my hand heals. I'd hate to have the blue mare think she's developed a new team ropin' technique."

Buck drove home with only one hand on the steering wheel. His right hand throbbed. He knew that taking some aspirin and an ice soak would help relieve some of the pain. He was disgusted with himself for not wearing his gloves. The worst part was the Missoula rodeo was coming up, and Tom was counting on him to be his roping partner. He wasn't going to be able to practice, and he wasn't even sure he would be healed enough to compete.

He pulled into the driveway and parked his rig next to the barn. He unloaded the mare and turned her out in the corral. For a moment he leaned against the fence, suddenly aware of his fatigue and the stiff pain he was beginning to feel in his shoulder. He didn't see or hear Ellie approaching him.

"Buck, I'm glad you are here. I was beginning to feel deserted. Uncle Ben went to one of the neighbors to look at a new bull he wants to buy. Everyone else seems to be gone, too." She stopped talking as she began to really see Buck. His face was dirty, and his shirt was torn.

Then she noticed his bandaged hand. "Buck, what happened?"

"I got careless, and the blue mare dumped me." He could see the concern in Ellie's eyes. Her apparent compassion for him filled him with tender longing. "I'm okay. I'm just a little bruised and rope-burned. I could use some aspirin and ice if you have any to spare."

Ellie grinned in spite of her concern. "Cowboys! You're such masters of understatement. Come up to the house. I have plenty of both. I want to hear all about what happened."

They went to the house, and Ellie had Buck sit down at the kitchen table. She got him some aspirin and then filled a mixing bowl with ice and cold water. "Here, let me help you with that."

She gently unwound the vet wrap from his bandaged hand. The raw burn looked red and oozed serum. Ellie swallowed hard and closed her eyes for a moment.

Buck put his hand gingerly into the ice cold water. He grimaced at the sting, but soon the numbing effect of the ice began to lessen the pain. He looked at Ellie in appreciation. "That feels much better. Thanks."

Buck and the Blue Roan

Ellie suddenly felt awkward. "Can I fix you a glass of iced tea and a sandwich?"

Buck squirmed in his chair, suddenly feeling like a trapped animal. He tried to sound nonchalant. "Only if you'll join me."

Ellie laughed self-consciously. "You know me. I'll use any excuse to eat."

She fixed the tea and sandwiches and sat down opposite Buck at the table. An awkward silence came between them. Ellie could not stand it any longer. "I think your hand has soaked long enough. I'll get some first aid cream to put on it, and then I can rewrap it for you."

Buck's brown eyes danced with good humor, glad for a break in the tension. "Thanks. I appreciate your help. Of course, if it's too much trouble, I could have the cook do it."

Ellie flared up. "What's he know about first aid?"

Buck didn't want to tell her the cook had more than likely patched up more cowboys than most doctors had. "Oh, probably nothin'," he lied.

"Well, then, I'd better do it."

Ellie left the kitchen to get her supplies. She returned shortly with a towel, scissors, cream, gauze and tape.

Buck grinned at her. "I bet you learned how to do this from watchin' those soap operas on TV."

"I'm certified in first aid. Do you want to see my card?"

Buck pulled his hand back with a look of feigned worry. "Yeah."

"Buck, you're impossible!" She pulled a chair close to his and sat down. She grabbed his wrist, pulled his hand to her and began to gently pat it dry with the towel. "This'll hurt, but it has to be thoroughly dried."

Buck spoke in a mock drawl. "I think I can take it, ma'am."

Ellie looked at Buck, and they both laughed. Controlling her amusement, she went back to work on his hand. She was intent on her work, her head bent. Buck could see the red-gold highlights shining in her thick hair. The soft fragrance of her perfume gently beckoned to him, filling him with an overwhelming desire to touch her hair, to hold her. Buck swallowed hard.

Ellie finished the last wrap of gauze and secured it with tape. "There, I'm done." She looked up into Buck's eyes. What she saw in the brown depths took her breath away. She got up quickly and took the bowl of ice water to the sink. Buck was standing in front of her when she turned around.

"Buck, I . . ."

Buck took her face in his hands and gently kissed her hair, her forehead and then her mouth. As his desire grew, he kissed her passionately. He had never wanted a girl this badly before. Suddenly, he froze.

Ellie looked up into his face. His expression was anguished, and his eyes were clouded with pain. "Buck, what's wrong?"

Buck pushed Ellie gently away. He struggled to gain control of his raging emotions. "I'm sorry, Ellie."

Ellie looked puzzled. "Don't you like me?"

Buck gritted his teeth, making his jaw ache. Yes, he liked her, but he couldn't be with her, not like this, not knowing what he knew. "Ellie, please try to understand. I do like you. You're the most beautiful girl I've ever known, but I can't compromise my beliefs, and I can't compromise you."

Ellie lashed out at him in frustration and anger. "Oh, Buck, you and your nerdy notions about purity and spirit helpers, I'm getting sick of it. Why don't you just go back to the reservation?"

With that, she left him and ran to her room. The slamming of her bedroom door punctuated the fact that this conversation was over.

Buck watched her go, the pain in his heart suddenly overpowering the pain in his hand. Slowly, he turned and walked out the back door. The cycle seemed to be coming full-circle. He vowed he would never make the same mistake his father had. Buck walked slowly down the hill to the bunkhouse.

♦♦♦

Ellie threw herself on her bed and sobbed. Hot tears ran down her cheeks and onto the old quilt. When her anger subsided, fear replaced it. She liked Buck; maybe she even loved him. She couldn't let these feelings happen, but part of her wanted his love . . . needed his love.

She recalled a conversation they had about Native Americans being warned by the tribal elders not to marry

Anglos; many believed they should be trying to bring back ethnic purity into their tribes. Buck told her when he got married it would be to a woman who loved him for who he was as a person more than anything else, but he also talked about the importance of his Flathead heritage and what it meant to future generations. It was not fair! No woman could love Buck more that she could if she wanted to, and his kiss . . . why did he kiss her like that unless he loved her, too? It certainly had not been a kiss of gratitude. Ellie gently touched her lips with her fingertips, remembering the thrill of being in Buck's arms. She rolled over and stared at the ceiling. "God, Great Spirit, whatev, if you're there, what do you want from me? Give me a sign, anything, just let me know you're real."

For a moment, Ellie held her breath, expecting a bolt of lightning or a spirit vision, or something, but her room remained quiet, the air still. She reached for the can of beer she had hidden in the tissue box beside her bed. She chided herself as she popped the top. "What a dork! Even if there is a god or a Great Spirit or whatevs, what does he care about me?"

THOU SHALT NOT STEAL

BEN RETURNED FROM HIS VISIT to the neighbors. Ellie had his dinner waiting for him. When he sat down, there was only one plate at the table. He looked at Ellie questioningly. "Aren't you going to eat, gal?"

Ellie avoided his gaze. "I ate a late lunch. I'm not hungry right now."

Ben smiled. "Well, at least stay and keep an old man company."

Ellie sat down reluctantly. Usually she enjoyed her time with Ben, but tonight she didn't feel like talking. Ben didn't seem to notice.

Ben didn't seem to notice. He talked about the neighbor's new bull. It was a breed name she did not recognize. He went on and on about the effects of crossbreeding and carcass evaluation and other aspects of the beef cattle business. Ellie couldn't keep her mind on what he was saying. She didn't have any idea what he was talking about, so finally, she excused herself. "Uncle Ben, I think I better go to bed. It's been a long day."

Ben looked intently at Ellie. "Go right ahead. Don't worry about the dishes. I'll tend to them."

Ellie got up from the table and gave Ben a hug. "Thanks, Uncle Ben. You're pretty dope."

Ben finished his dinner, gathered his plates and took them to the sink. He noticed the two sets of dishes in the basin and smiled. There was only one other person besides himself who would have eaten lunch in his house, and that person was Buck. He spoke quietly to himself. "Hang in there, cowboy. You'll win her heart yet."

♦♦♦

Ellie was exhausted and emotionally drained, but she couldn't sleep. She tossed and turned for an hour. Finally, she flung back the covers and got up. She thought maybe a walk outside would clear her mind, so she dressed, grabbed her coat and quietly left the house.

The late summer nights were getting cold. During her stay with Ben, she'd come to realize what good listeners horses could be, so she headed for the corrals. It was dark, but the moon was clearing the horizon, giving a ghostly pale light to the barnyard.

She went to the haystack and reached between the bales of hay, comforted by the cool, smooth aluminum as it touched her fingertips. She pulled a can out of the six-pack and popped the top. The tangy smell of the beer tickled her nose, and she took a long, grateful drink. After a few more sips, she headed for the corral, but as she rounded the corner of the barn she heard a voice. Instinctively, she pulled back into the shadows. Someone else was out with the horses. Ellie held her breath, listening. She recognized the voice. It was Buck. She stuck her head around the corner, straining to hear what he was saying. It became apparent he, too, was seeking comfort from the horses. As her eyes adjusted to the dim light, she could see him in the corral with the blue mare.

Buck stood close to the mare, cradling her head in his arms and rubbing her forehead. "This has been some day, horse. First, you take your frustration out on me, and then Ellie lets me have it. Maybe I deserved it. Here I thought she'd be mad at me for kissin' her, but it turns out she got mad because I stopped. Things sure do get complicated with women."

Heat rose up in Ellie's face. She felt guilty for eavesdropping and shame for her earlier behavior. Ellie turned to sneak away before Buck discovered her. As she did, she tripped over a large rock and fell into some buckets by the side of the barn, spilling what was left of the beer all over her jeans. The crash made a terrible noise, which brought Buck over the fence and around the barn in a matter of seconds. Ellie struggled to get up as Buck grabbed her by the coat collar and spun her around. He had his fist drawn back, ready for a fight; the moon shining on his face made him look wild and fierce.

Ellie gasped. "Buck, don't. It's me, Ellie."

"Ellie! What are you doin' here?" Buck looked horrified by the realization of what he had almost done. He let go of her coat and backed away. "I thought you were someone tryin' to steal saddles."

Ellie tried to put more distance between her and Buck. "It's okay. I guess I came down here for the same reason you did. I couldn't sleep, so I thought a talk with the horses might help."

The smell of beer crashed into Buck's senses and filled him with a familiar disgust. "It looks to me like you came down here for more than a talk with the horses."

The anger in his voice shocked Ellie. She dropped the beer can she was holding as it if were a hot potato and sat down against the barn. "Buck, I just needed a drink to help me relax. I don't drink much . . . Honest."

Buck picked up a rock and threw it at the water-trough. The loud clank of it hitting the metal spooked the horses. They snorted and milled around the corral restlessly. "Darn it, Ellie. Don't lie to me. I found your stash in the haystack a long time ago, and I've smelled beer on your breath more times than I can remember. Why are you pulling such a dumb stunt?"

Confused, Ellie sat silent for a moment. She really had no answer to Buck's question, and his attitude was starting to make her mad. Finally, she snapped at him. "I don't know, and I don't care. Besides, who do you think you are judging me? It's none of your business what I do."

Ellie pushed herself up and started to walk past Buck on her way back to the house. Buck reached out and grabbed

Buck and the Blue Roan

her arm, squeezing it so hard Ellie cried out in pain. She tried to pull away. "Let go of me!"

Buck pushed her roughly up against the barn wall. "You know, I really don't care what you think of me, but you're going to stay put until you hear what I have to say. Now sit down and shut up!"

Shocked, Ellie did what she was told; she sat down and looked at Buck pacing back and forth in front of her like a caged lion. His black hair glistened in the moonlight, making him look unreal. She couldn't have spoken even if she'd wanted to because she felt a fear she'd never known before constrict her throat.

Buck finally stopped pacing and stood in front of her. "How can you do this to Ben? He's been the greatest to you, and you repay him by sneaking around behind his back stealing beer from the cook shack. Do you even have any idea what you're doin' to yourself and to the people around you? Do you?"

Buck kneeled down in front of Ellie and grabbed her shoulders, bringing his face close to hers. "Well, do you?"

Tears welled in Ellie's eyes, and she shook her head. She whispered in a small voice, "No."

Buck let her go and sat down cross-legged in front of her. He let out a long sigh. "Well then, let me tell you what you're doin'. You're playin' a dangerous game with yourself and your children comin' down the road. My mother was just like you. She drank a little, and then she married my dad. When he went off to the Gulf War, he left her pregnant, and she started drinkin' a whole lot more. Because of her drinkin' my older brother, Rusty, was born with Fetal Alcohol Syndrome. Every time I look at him, I think of how it would be if he was normal, and then I think about how he was made the way he is. The alcohol destroyed his chances of enjoyin' his life and his family the way he could have, and all because my mother wouldn't admit she had a drinkin' problem."

Ellie was stunned. "Buck, I'm so sorry. I don't know what to say."

Buck sat quietly for what seemed like minutes before he spoke. "Don't say anything, Ellie. Just stop your drinkin' before it's too late."

He leaned over and kissed her lightly on the cheek. "Good night. I'm sorry if I hurt you."

He jumped to his feet and walked away before she could reply. Ellie made no effort to move. She sat with her back against the barn and thought about Buck's words as she looked up at the stars. She felt sorry for Buck, but she thought he was over-reacting. She knew she didn't have a drinking problem.

The moon was setting behind the Bitterroots when Ellie finally got stiffly to her feet and headed for the house.

♦♦♦

Buck went to bed worried about the tension that was continuing to grow between himself and Ellie, and he was even more troubled by his feelings for her. He knew from experience the hardest task would be to get her to admit to her alcohol abuse, and the chances of that happening were slim to none. He thought about it all the next day, and in the weeks to come. When his rope burn healed enough to start practicing again, he was less than the quick roper Tom was used to having as his partner.

After Buck had missed his second and third steer, Tom rode up beside him. "Hey, partner, are you an astronaut or a heeler?"

Buck looked at him blankly. "Huh?"

"You seem to be out in space today."

"I'm sorry. I just can't concentrate."

Tom looked at him knowingly. "You need to talk about it?"

Buck shrugged. "Yeah, I guess so."

Buck and Tom tied their horses to the fence and sat down. Tom waited patiently for Buck to gather his thoughts. Finally, Buck sighed. "It's Ellie."

"What's wrong with Ellie?" Tom's concern shone in his voice.

"Nothin's wrong with her. It's me. Tom, I think I'm in love with her." Buck spoke as if he was announcing his own death sentence.

Tom began to chuckle. Buck looked up in surprise. "What's so funny?"

"Nothin', except everyone but you has known it for a long time. How come it took you so long to figure it out?"

"What do you mean?"

"Buck, it's been written all over you for weeks: the way you look at her, the way you talk about her, the way you try to protect her."

Buck looked chagrined, and then he became serious. "Tom, don't you see the problem? We're from different worlds and different cultures, and there's something else. I think Ellie's an alcoholic. Our relationship is a dead end."

Tom's heart ached for Buck. "Relax, kid. Trust your heart; listen to your instincts."

"That doesn't give me much hope because my instincts are tellin' me to run as far from this situation as I can."

Tom could hear the bitterness in Buck's voice. "Are you still blamin' your dad for everything that's gone wrong in your life?"

Old feelings welled up inside Buck and spilled over. "If Dad loved me so much, why did he let one of the most important things in my life slip away? And now I'm in love with a girl who's hooked on booze. So tell me why I shouldn't blame him."

Tom decided to take the bull by the horns. "Buck, I'm going to tell you some things that will probably make you mad, so if you feel like punchin' me go ahead. If you're honest with yourself, you'll see your thinkin's pretty childish. Everybody suffers losses. It's one of the hazards of livin', and we all make choices: some good, some bad. You can keep blamin' others for your miseries or you can take control of your life and make a difference in this world. It's rotten what happened to your mother, but she made her own choices, too. Maybe your dad could have saved her;

maybe he couldn't. Maybe it's your purpose to keep Ellie from following your mother's path."

Tom drew a deep breath and braced himself. He'd been punched for less, and by some of his best friends.

Buck was silent for a long time. Finally, he spoke. "Tom, do you think it'll ever go away?"

Tom looked a little confused, but he thought he would give the question a try. "No, but it would help if you quit fightin' the memory of your parents' death. It seems to me you have a lot of forgivin' to do: your dad, your mom, your grandfather . . . and yourself. Now, if you feel up to it, let's do some ropin'."

♦♦♦

Summer was running out of time. The days were still hot, but the evenings were getting crisp and cold, hinting at the coming of fall to the Bitterroots.

Ellie spent her days in the fields helping with the second cutting of hay. Buck was busy putting the finishing touches on the three-year-olds. Several had been sold over the summer. The remaining few would be consigned to a fall Quarter Horse sale.

The roping season had been good to Buck and Tom. They'd both won buckles and more than enough money to meet their expenses, but the season had been marred. The saddle stealing continued with reports of missing saddles coming in from all over the state. Leads were few and seemed impossible to follow.

Eric Vance was being a model citizen. He always had an alibi, and he made a point of going out of his way to be nice to Buck and Tom.

Morgan, on the other hand, looked as if she could spit venom every time she saw them. The atmosphere was electric with possibilities. It was time for one of the biggest rodeos of the season.

Buck and Tom stood a good chance of winning the team roping if they didn't have any more accidents. Buck was roping on the blue mare. He wanted to find out if she could take the pressure of competition. She was coming along good. In spite of her occasional temper tantrums, she and Buck were finally starting to work as a team. He hadn't been bucked off in three weeks.

Now, the day of the rodeo, Ben and Ellie were going to Missoula with Buck. Tom had some work he had to do, so he was coming later. Buck put his gear in the trailer and loaded the mare. He looked up at the sky. It was overcast with dark gray clouds, heavy with moisture. Rain! He hated roping in the rain.

He saw Ellie and Ben coming from the house. "I hope you two brought your rain gear. It looks like we're going to get wet before the day's over."

Ellie glanced up. The sky looked ominously gray. "I think you're right. Could you wait a minute while I go back for my coat?"

"Sure, but hurry."

Ben had already reached the truck. His coat was under his arm. He grinned at Buck. "I think she had other things on her mind."

Tom's words came back to Buck. He knew what Ben was thinking. His face flushed hot, as he tried to cover his embarrassment. "Women! It seems like a guy always has to wait for them."

Ben smiled knowingly. "You better get used to it."

Buck shook his head in protest. "No, I'm not ready for that. Not now. Maybe never."

"Now, it's not that bad. A good woman can be a great comfort." Ben tried to encourage Buck.

Ellie returned with her coat and a blanket. She looked apologetically at Buck as she climbed in the truck beside him. Ben got in after her, and they were on their way.

It was about an hour's drive; a drive that passed in silence.

Buck pulled his rig into the Missoula fairgrounds and found a place to park. It was crowded with people coming to see the fair and rodeo. He made sure he wasn't where he could get boxed in by other trucks before he turned to Ben and Ellie. "Why don't you two look around at the exhibits while I saddle up and get the mare settled?"

Ben looked at Ellie questioningly. "What do you want to do?"

"That'll be fine. We can always meet back here later."

Ben and Ellie left Buck to care for his mare and pay his entry fees. They wove their way through the large crowd that was milling around the exhibit barns. The threat of bad weather did not seem to dampen the festive atmosphere of the fair. Ellie loved it. "Uncle Ben, this is sick?" She hugged him right there in front of everyone.

◆◆◆

Buck took his time saddling the mare. Her nerves were on edge with the storm coming in. He knew he was going to have to give her a long warm up period or he might as well enter the saddle bronc riding, too. She had never seen so many cars or horses either. Her head was up, and she tested the wind for signs of danger. Buck watched her with admiration. "You better get used to it, sis. I hope to have a long and successful ropin' career with you."

After he paid his fees, Buck went to look at the exhibits. It was pointless to try to find Ben and Ellie. He would either run into them accidentally, or they would meet him back at the trailer. The "elephant ears" stand caught his attention. Buck had a weakness for the crisp, hot cinnamon sugar pastry. He ordered one and a cup of black coffee and sat down to enjoy himself. The coffee tasted good, and its heat warmed him. The temperature was dropping. Montana had a strange way of mixing seasons. Snow in late August was not unheard of in the mountains. Buck shivered. It was time to warm up the mare. Tom should be arriving soon, and they needed to find out what they could about the steer they drew for the team roping. It was going to be a tough roping. Any advantage they could get would be a help.

Buck and the Blue Roan

Buck got up, wiped the crumbs from his mouth, walked back to his rig, his thoughts occupied with the upcoming roping. He didn't pay much attention to the police car parked next to his truck. There were usually several deputies patrolling a fair and rodeo. It wasn't until he saw the officer walking around his rig that he became alarmed. The first thought that entered his mind was that his saddle had been stolen.

As he approached the trailer, the officer stepped forward. "Are you Buck Eagle Plume?"

Something about the officer's body language made Buck wary. "Yes. What's going on here?"

The man ignored Buck's question. "Is this your rig?"

"Yes, but what's . . . ?"

"Will you please open the front compartment of your trailer?"

"Sure." Buck opened the tack compartment of his trailer. An unfamiliar saddle was sitting on the saddle rack. It was not Tom's saddle. "I wonder where this came from."

"Put your hands on the truck and spread your legs!"

Buck complied while the officer quickly searched him for a weapon. Dazed, Buck hoped this was all just a bad dream.

The officer removed a pair of handcuffs from his belt. Buck felt the cold steel bite into his wrist. "You have the right to remain silent. You have the right . . ."

The words jarred Buck out of his stupor, and he suddenly felt angry and scared all at the same time. "I know my rights. Will you please tell me what's going on?"

Eric Vance stepped out from behind Buck's trailer. "It's simple friend. You're being arrested for the theft of a saddle. My saddle." He opened the tack compartment again. Now Buck recognized the saddle inside. It belonged to Eric Vance.

The young cowboy went cold inside. "You know I didn't steal your saddle. You'll never get away with this Vance."

Eric looked apologetically at the police officer and shrugged his shoulders. Then he turned on Buck, steel daggers dancing in the depths of his brown eyes. "Can you prove you didn't steal my saddle?"

Buck thought of the past hour he'd spent alone. He had no alibi. It was Vance's word against his. Icy fingers of fear squeezed his heart. He turned to the officer. "Let me get ahold of my friends, so I can tell them what's going on."

The officer took out a pen and notepad. "This isn't a social visit. You'll get your phone call when we get downtown. I'll leave a note on your truck telling your friends where they can find you. I'd like to have a little chat with them myself."

The officer scribbled a hurried note and stuck it under the wiper blade on Buck's truck before he shoved him unceremoniously into the back of the waiting patrol car.

The gray sky opened up, starting with huge drops of water that gradually built momentum into a steady downpour.

Spirit Helper

THE RAIN FELL in a steady drizzle. Tom eyed Buck's wet saddle and horse. Something was wrong, and it worried him. The blue mare had pawed a hole in the ground in front of her. The dirt she dug up was rapidly turning to mud. Where was Buck? It was not like him to miss the warm up or to leave his horse this way.

Tom left Buck's rig and hurried to the rodeo office to see if they had seen Buck. The rodeo secretary told him Buck had been there an hour and a half ago. Tom hoped Buck was just taking in the sights of the fair with Ben and Ellie and had lost track of time, but he should have been back by now.

Tom returned to his own rig, hoping that Buck would be there waiting for him. He had already warmed up his horse and put him back in the trailer to keep him from getting wet and chilled. He reached over the tailgate and patted the horse's rump. "Take it easy, fella. I'll be back as soon as I find our partner."

Reaching into the front of his pickup, Tom got his slicker and put it on. This rain was a soaker. He headed for the exhibit buildings. Maybe he would find Buck there. Tom had not gone far when he saw Ben and Ellie emerging from the crowd. He waved, and they waved back. As they approached, he asked, "Where's Buck?"

Ellie's dark hair hung in damp strands from beneath her rain hat. She looked radiant and happy. "We were just on our way to meet him at his truck. Tom could not help admiring Ellie, his fears lost for the moment in the presence of her beauty. She even looked good with wet, straggly hair. He thought that Buck was lucky to have this girl for a friend, which reminded him . . ."Buck's not at his rig. I've looked all over for him. I was hopin' he was with you."

Ben did not appear to be worried. "He probably got cold and went for a cup of coffee. We'll just wait for him in his truck. He'll show up."

Tom looked doubtful. "I don't know. If he doesn't get back soon and warm up his horse, he'll be in for more rodeo than he bargained for. "

The three of them sat in the front of Buck's truck. They made small talk for thirty minutes. The rodeo was under way in spite of the rain. The windows of the truck fogged over. Ellie leaned forward to turn on the defroster. As she did, she noticed the piece of paper stuck under the wiper blade. "I wonder what that is."

Tom grinned. "Buck's probably the first cowboy in history to get a parkin' ticket at a rodeo."

Ellie got out of the truck and gingerly lifted the wiper blade, removing the soggy piece of paper, but she did not attempt to look at it until she got back in the truck. Then she slipped her fingernails between the wet edges and gently peeled them apart. The blurred ink was hard to read, and Ellie could not make sense of it. She handed the paper to Ben. He took the note and read it, his eyes squinted almost shut. He reached across Ellie and handed the note to Tom. Tom could see by Ben's expression it was not good news. The note did not make sense. Buck was at the rodeo, not at the city jail. He had not said anything about having business downtown.

Ellie looked at Ben, at Tom and then back to Ben. "What's wrong? Where's Buck?"

♦♦♦

The patrol car door shut with a dull thud. Buck sat in the back seat, his cuffed hands behind him, digging into his spine. Surely this nightmare would soon be over, and he would be roping with Tom. But he knew this was not a dream. Eric Vance had set him up, and it was a simple, deadly plan.

Buck stared out the window of the moving patrol car, trying to figure a way out of this mess. He had no defense, no alibi, and he knew there was no way he could prove he didn't steal Vance's saddle. He was sure Vance had left a clever trail of clues that would point to him as the guilty party. Buck felt vulnerable and hopeless.

The trip to the city jail was short. The steady downpour had turned to a drizzling rain. The officer parked the patrol car, got out, and opened the back door. "Come on, buddy; the free ride is over."

Buck looked into the face of the unsympathetic deputy. He wanted to strike out at this man who was accusing him unjustly, but he knew it would only get him deeper in trouble. Instead, he looked the man straight in the eyes. "Thank you for your consideration."

The officer dropped his gaze and mumbled something inaudible before he shoved Buck toward the door. "You'll get what's comin' to you, hot shot. You Indians are all alike."

The booking procedure humiliated Buck even more. His pocket knife, watch and billfold were taken from him and put in a large manila envelope. After that, another officer fingerprinted him and took his picture. The man who booked him looked at Buck as if he was a nonentity. "You can have your phone call now."

Buck was not sure who to call. Anyone who could help him would be at the rodeo; even his grandfather and Rusty were coming. No one carried a cell phone. Finally, he picked up the receiver and dialed Gordon's number. The phone rang several times before someone picked it up. Buck's face brightened at the sound of a friendly voice.

"Hello. Mrs. Ritter, this is Buck Eagle Plume. When Gordon gets home, will you tell him I'm in the city jail in Missoula? Have him make sure Tom knows about it. No. No. It's just a little misunderstandin'. I'll be okay. Thanks."

He put the receiver slowly back on the hook. This was not just a little misunderstanding, and he knew it. Buck sighed as a dark cloud of despair settled over him. He hoped Ben and Ellie had gotten the officer's note; yet, the thought of them seeing him like this made him flush with shame.

The booking officer broke in on his thoughts. "It's lock-up time. Since you won't be arraigned until Monday, you'll have to spend a couple of nights with us."

Another officer led Buck down the hall. The worn linoleum floor bore testimony that many men had made that same journey. Buck's footsteps echoed hollowly as he and his escort approached the lock-up area.

The officer nodded to a guard who unlocked the steel door before them. A blast of fetid air hit Buck in the face; the smell of urine and vomit was faintly masked by the odor of disinfectant. The officer opened a cell whose sole occupant was a drunken vagrant. He motioned Buck inside, and then locked the door and left. The outer door closed with a sickening thud of finality.

Buck took hold of the bars in front of him, squeezing them until the veins on the backs of his hands stood out. He rested his head on his forearm. Anguish contorted his face as he groaned in despair. *Why now; why this?*

The drunk stirred momentarily and looked at Buck. He swayed slightly as he tried to focus on his new roommate. "Hey, fella, ya gotta drink on ya?"

♦♦♦

Tom loaded the blue mare in his trailer along with the gray, then locked Buck's rig. The three friends drove to the police station in silence, each one lost in speculation about what was happening to Buck. Ellie's imagination ran wild. She hoped Buck had caught the saddle thief and had to go to the station to sign a statement. Or maybe he had found a lost child, or maybe . . . it went on and on.

After what seemed like an eternity to Ellie, Tom pulled into a parking spot at the station. The three occupants of the pickup hurried into the building with an urgency that belied their outward calm. Tom held the door for Ellie and Ben. They stopped just inside the door, their eyes searching the room for Buck. He was nowhere in sight.

Tom approached the officer at the desk. "Excuse me, but we're lookin' for a friend of ours. Someone left us a note sayin' he would be here."

The officer looked up from the paperwork he had before him. "What's this friend's name?"

Tom continued to look around the room as he spoke. "Buck Eagle Plume."

The officer's attitude of disinterest suddenly changed. "You say you're friends of his?"

Ben stepped forward. "He works for me."

"Well, you'd better be lookin' for a new hand because this friend of yours was just booked on felony charges for grand theft."

The three of them stood stunned. Tom spoke under his breath. "This is worse than I thought."

Ben and Tom exchanged a look that drove a pang of fear into Ellie's heart. She grabbed Ben's arm. "Ben?"

Ben tried to sound encouraging. "It's all right, Ellie. There's just been some misunderstandin'. We'll get this straightened out in a jiffy."

Tom turned back to the officer. "What is it Buck is supposed to have stolen?"

"A saddle, maybe several saddles, and we have a witness that can identify Mr. Eagle Plume as the thief."

An inner fear caused Tom to lose his patience. His cool tone belied his growing frustration. "And just who is this witness?"

"I can't give you that information." The officer went back to his work, making it clear that the interview was over.

Tom fought to control his rising anger. Ben could see what was coming. He stepped forward. "Could we please see Mr. Eagle Plume for a few moments? We need to find out what to do with his horse and rig."

The officer looked up, trying to judge the man standing before him. "I guess it'll be okay, but you can only have a few minutes."

Ben, trying to defuse the tense situation, smiled in appreciation. "Thanks. A few minutes is all we need."

Tom, Ben and Ellie were escorted to the visitor's area. They were seated at a table. After several nerve-wracking minutes, a door opened, and Buck was escorted into the room by a guard. When Ellie saw him, the love for Buck she had been trying to deny swept over her. Her eyes sought his, and through sheer will, she tried to express the feelings she dared not say out loud.

Tom cleared his throat as Buck sat down across the table from them. Buck held out his hand to Ellie, his shame and humiliation clouding the depths of his brown eyes.

The guard stepped forward. "No touching!"

Ellie pulled back her small hand. "It's all right, Buck. It doesn't matter to me that you're in here because I know you didn't steal that saddle . . . you couldn't."

Buck looked into Ellie's green eyes, his heart full of painful longing. "Thanks."

Tom leaned forward. "I hate to interrupt you two, but do you mind tellin' us what happened?"

As Buck related the events of his day, Tom couldn't hold back the question burning in his mind. "Who's this supposed witness they have?"

Buck swallowed hard as he tried to gain control of his emotions. "Eric Vance."

For the second time that day, Tom, Ben and Ellie were stunned into silence, but silence was not in Tom's nature. He found his voice. "What?"

Buck sighed. "It was Vance's saddle they found in my trailer, and he was right there to tell them I stole it."

Tom shook his head in disgust. "Are they blind? Can't they see it's a setup?"

Buck appreciated his friend's frustration. "Tom, they're just doin' their job. All the evidence points to me. What else are they supposed to believe?"

Tom pounded the table with his fist. "When I get my hands on Eric Vance, I'm going to . . ."

The guard motioned to Buck. "Time's up. Let's go."

Ben spoke up. "I'll see about posting bail.

"Thanks, Ben, but I won't be arraigned until Monday. It looks like I'm stuck here for a couple of nights. Could you please fill Grandfather in on what's going on?"

Tom tipped his hat to Buck. "Hang in there, partner. We'll get you out of this mess. That's a promise."

Ben said his goodbyes and got up to leave. Ellie sat frozen to the chair, her eyes brimming with tears. Buck looked back over his shoulder and smiled weakly. "Hey, it's going to be all right."

♦♦♦

Ellie's mind swam in a dark ocean of whirling emotions. The trip from Missoula to the ranch passed in a blur. When they got home, she excused herself and went to her room. Tom and Ben let her go without saying anything. She hung up her rain gear, then sat down numbly on her bed.

Ellie wanted to cry, to scream, to throw things at the wall, but all she could do was sit and stare at the floor. What if Buck was convicted and sent to prison? But she told herself that that could not happen because the law was fair and just. He would be found innocent of any crime. She knew, however, that Eric Vance was counting on "blind justice" to destroy Buck. Fear rushed over her and threatened to suffocate her.

Ellie felt trapped and utterly helpless. Why had she played games with Buck? Why hadn't she told him how she really felt about him? A dull aching pain filled her chest as she began to realize just how much she did love him. Now she felt that if she lost him, she would die. She cried in anguish to an unknown power. "Oh, God, if you are there, please help him. And please . . . Help me!"

With the coming of night, Ellie fell into a restless sleep. She was still dressed and lying on top of the covers. During the night, her mind sank deeper into darkness. She felt cold and alone, and terror at being isolated in this darkness. Ellie ran, looking for the light. Suddenly, there appeared a hand reaching for her out of the darkness. At last, someone had come to rescue her! She grabbed desperately for the hand, and now she had it, but something was wrong. She was caught in its grasp, and she could not let go. The hand was cold, so very cold, and it was pulling her down, down . . . down into the darkness. Ellie tried to scream, but her throat was constricted by terror. Her mind voiced what her mouth could not. *Somebody, please help me!*

Just as she felt herself about to swoon, she heard a strange noise. The sound of a voice singing a lullaby came to her, and she opened her eyes to see a beautiful blue-white light. Ellie reached out with her free hand and cried. "Mother? !"

A figure approached her out of the light, but it was not her mother. The woman moved with the grace of a swan as she stretched out her hand to Ellie. The flowing white robe she wore rippled with her every move, and her golden hair shone with the brightness of the noonday sun. As the woman drew closer, Ellie felt the warmth of her tender smile, and saw compassion in the sapphire blue eyes. The graceful fingertips of the woman's slender hand beckoned.

Ellie woke trembling and sweating with her mouth dry and her heart pounding. The nightmare seemed so real. She could not get the feeling of sinking, of being cold and alone out of her mind. She wondered if this was Hell: the total isolation, this separation from everything and everyone she loved.

Even more troubling was the vision of the woman. Who could she be? Ellie started to reach for her hidden can of beer, but Buck's words came back to her with sudden clarity. What was she doing?

She got up and went to the kitchen. Ellie hoped some hot chocolate would settle her nerves. She put the tea kettle on the stove and was glad that it did not take the water long to boil. The familiar whistle brought her comfort. This was reality, something she could rely on. She poured the boiling water in the chocolate mix and sat down at the table. Her spoon made a tiny whirlpool in the dark liquid as she stirred and stirred.

Ben appeared in the doorway. "I see you couldn't sleep either."

Ellie nodded her head in agreement. "Uncle Ben, I'm afraid. I feel so helpless."

"I know." Ben sat down and squeezed Ellie's hand. "We'll go see Buck in the morning."

Something else nagged at the back of Ellie's mind and caused her to sigh deeply. Ben noticed. "Do you want to talk about what's really botherin' you?"

She looked up in surprise, then flushed because she feared Ben could read her expression. There was a moment before she gathered the courage to speak. "Uncle Ben, what do you know about Buck's mother?"

Ellie hedged around the truth. "He just told me she had some problems with drinking. I was wondering if you knew about it."

Ben sighed, and his eyes filled with sadness. "It's not a very pretty story, and I'm not sure I should be tellin' it."

Ellie grabbed Ben's arm in a tight grip, and a desperate look came into her eyes. "Please tell me. I need to know."

Ben looked into Ellie's eyes and then down at the white knuckles of the hand grasping his arm. He didn't know why, but he felt he should tell her.

"Buck's mom and dad died in a drunk driving car accident on Highway 93 when he was just a little boy. The drunk driver was Buck's mom. His dad had just gotten back from the Gulf War. When he left, Buck's mom started drinkin' real heavy until she became a full-fledged alcoholic. Then she had Rusty. When Buck's dad signed up for a second tour of duty, his mom came completely unglued."

Ellie prodded Ben to continue. "What happened?"

Ben was not used to talking so much. He took a sip of hot chocolate and gathered his thoughts. "She got pregnant

Buck and the Blue Roan

with Buck when Ed Eagle Plume was home on leave. The neighbors tried to help her as much as they could because the house was a mess and the kids were pretty neglected. When Ed came home, he had to get a job in Missoula to keep the ranch going and to pay for Rusty's home care. His Fetal Alcohol Syndrome left him with a lot of problems. Somewhere in all of the confusion, Buck kind of got lost. After his folks were killed, his grandpa came to live with them. All I know is it's a rotten way for a kid to have to grow up."

Ellie suddenly felt hot and nauseated, but she tried to remain calm because she didn't want Ben to see how much his story frightened her. She got up slowly and put her mug in the sink. "I guess I better get back to bed now. Thanks, Uncle Ben."

"That's a good idea. It's going to be a long weekend. I talked to Buck's grandfather. He'll be at the hearing." Ben got up and left for his bedroom; Ellie rinsed their mugs out and put them in the drying rack.

Sleep didn't come easy to Ellie. She couldn't get the haunting picture of Buck standing behind bars out of her mind, but even more tormenting was the image of a little boy standing at the graveside of his dead parents. When at last the alarm went off, Ellie welcomed the obnoxious buzz. She was not sure she had even slept at all.

She spent longer than usual in the shower, letting the hot water pound the fatigue from her neck and shoulders. The heat and the steam left her feeling somewhat refreshed and a bit more relaxed. She toweled off briskly, then went to the closet to pick out a dress. Ellie hadn't worn one all summer, and Buck had never seen her in a dress. Well, he would today.

Ben whistled his appreciation when Ellie walked into the kitchen. "You sure are a pretty sight for a tired old man, or any man for that matter."

Ellie blushed. "Thanks. I thought it might cheer Buck to see me in something besides faded old jeans."

The dress felt uncomfortable; Ellie squirmed in the seat of the truck. Ben looked at her questioningly, so Ellie looked down to avoid his eyes. The taste of beer lingered in her mouth. She felt ashamed, a feeling she was experiencing more and more. She needed to talk because she didn't want to think anymore. Ellie said the first thing that came to her mind. "Uncle Ben, what did Buck's mom look like?"

Ben gave Ellie an odd look. "She was a blue-eyed blond.

To Catch a Thief

OCCASIONAL FITS OF COUGHING interrupted the drunk's loud snoring. Buck tossed and turned, trying to find a comfortable position on the small bunk in his cell. Even without the noise, he wouldn't have been able to sleep. For a moment, he envied the drunk's oblivion. Buck's mind whirled with questions. Why was he in this mess? How was he ever going to get out of it? What would his grandfather say? He could only guess that his grandfather would take the Marine Corp approach, and he would expect Buck to handle the situation like a man. Buck remembered Tom's words about his need to be able to forgive. Could he ever get rid of his feelings of anger and bitterness?

Thoughts of his parents flooded his memory. Buck fought back the stinging tears that came to his eyes. Now was not the time for self-pity. He had to work this out, alone, before he could ever deal with forgiving anyone. His emotional battle raged through the night. He paced the floor, then lay down, only to get right back up and pace some more.

All of the commotion finally woke the drunk. He watched the young cowboy pacing back and forth like a mountain lion. Fear started to show in the old drunk's bleary eyes. He expressed his concern in a shaky voice. "Say, fella, you're not wound up on drugs are ya? I mean . . . can I get ya some help or somethin'?"

Buck looked grim. "You're right. I need help, but not the kind you're thinking of. Go back to sleep."

The rheumy blue eyes of the older man started to water from the effort of trying to focus as he studied Buck pacing the floor. "Ya know, I used to be like you once."

Buck stopped his pacing to look at the old man. On closer inspection, Buck guessed the drunk was older than he appeared, maybe the same age as his grandfather. Matted gray hair stuck out from under a stocking cap that was so filthy it was impossible to tell what its original color had been. Deep creases crisscrossed the landscape of his face, and the stubble of his beard showed like dirty snow. Buck figured he would not be able to sleep, so he may as well humor his new roommate. "How's that?"

Buck's words startled the drunk back from whatever place he'd slipped into for the moment. "Huh? What's that?"

Buck sighed and sat down on his bunk. He leaned towards the drunk. "I asked, how were you once like me?"

The older man seemed to consider the question a long time before he finally answered. "I was good lookin' and full of fire just like you. That was before the war."

His curiosity piqued, Buck prodded the man to continue. "What war?"

The drunk turned his head ever so slightly and looked into Buck's eyes. "The Vietnam War."

The words seemed to hang in the air like a dark storm cloud. Neither of the jail cell's occupants spoke for a long time. Finally, Buck couldn't stand the heavy silence any longer. "What did you do there?"

A frightening intensity came into the drunk's voice. "I served on a helicopter Medivac team. We were known as the tag 'em and bag 'em squad. We ended up doing more recovery than rescue. Ya wanna know what that's like? Well, I'll tell ya."

"One time it took us half a week to get to the guys because the ground fire was so intense. By the time we got there, the Marines had run the Cong off, but we lost most of our men. We put 'er down in the LZ and had to walk into the swamp lookin' for bodies."

"They were everywhere around us, just floatin' in the water like great big camouflaged fishin' bobbers. The methane gas had 'em swelled up so they were tight as drums. One of the new guys made the mistake of touchin' one of 'em. Right then the trapped gas started to leach out, and the kid lost his lunch."

Buck swallowed hard. He'd seen enough dead cattle to know what week-old death looked and smelled like. While the gruesome image swam in his mind, the old soldier continued.

"Then there was this guy . . . We were in a hot LZ and movin' fast
. . . just throwin' bodies in the helicopter . . . we'd sort them later. When we got back to the base, the guys started a parts pile—limbs we couldn't identify. One of the guys picked up this big hunk of flesh and threw it off the helicopter onto the pile. That's when it started to make a weird gurgling noise. I took a closer look . . . it was a *live* Marine. He must have stepped on a mine because he was missin' all of his extremities, his groin and his face. The heat from the blast had cauterized all of his blood vessels, leavin' the poor guy trapped in a living hell. They kept him alive for a week. Maybe they were hopin' he would utter his name through his crushed trachea, so they could ID him for the family. Maybe . . ."

Buck looked on in horror as the old drunk started chuckling. The chuckling grew into hysterical laughter, which finally ended in choking sobs. Buck flopped over on his bunk, turned his face to the wall and tried to shut out the sounds of a war he could never forget. The eastern horizon showed rose pink as the sun finally climbed over the mountains. Only a few gray cloud fragments were left as testimony of yesterday's storm. Buck felt like he'd been run over by a herd of wild horses. He looked over at his roommate, who was holding his head in obvious pain. Was his grandfather locked in this same unending nightmare?

♦♦♦

Buck and the Blue Roan

The steel door swung open on complaining hinges. Buck's mind faintly registered the noise, then rejected it as he fought to keep his hold on the sleep that had finally come to him. The jailer's voice barely broke through the barrier. "Hey, wake up. You got visitors. Let's go."

Buck grimaced. "Can I at least wash my face?"

The jailer nodded. "Sure, but don't take too long."

Buck quickly slapped water on his face and ran his fingers through his matted hair. The jailer opened the door and once more escorted him to the visiting area. Tom and Ben were sitting at the table. He wondered where Ellie was, but he was also glad she wasn't there to see him in his wretched state.

Tom grinned at Buck. "You look awful."

The full realization hit Buck of how special his roping partner was. He expressed his feelings like a true cowboy. "You're not so good lookin' yourself, ya know."

Tom laughed. "All right, I give up. How'd it go last night?"

Buck yawned. "Rough. My roommate gave me a history lesson that helped me see my grandfather and his Vietnam experience in a whole different light."

Tom looked intently at Buck. "I was wonderin' when that was going to happen. I'm glad to see you're growin' up."

Buck grinned sheepishly. "You've had a lot to do with that, Tom, and I'm grateful."

"What are friends for?"

Ben cleared his throat. "How's it going, cowboy?"

Buck sighed. "Not bad, but I'll be glad to get out of here." While he spoke, his eyes searched the room for Ellie. Finally, he couldn't hold back the question burning in his mind, but he tried to sound indifferent. "Where's Ellie?"

Ben smiled. "She's waitin' outside. She wanted to talk to you alone. Tom and I'll be seein' you tomorrow."

Ben and Tom left the room. Buck longed to see Ellie, but his experience of the night before made their relationship seem even more impossible than before. He had a long way to go with his relationship with his grandfather, and he wasn't even sure where to start. Now he had to deal with Vance's accusations. He just didn't have anything left emotionally to invest in a risky romance. Well, at least they could be friends . . . or could they? He waited impatiently. The outside door opened as another guard escorted Ellie to the table. As soon as Ellie stepped into the room, Buck was struck by her appearance. "Ellie!"

Ellie was startled by the tone of Buck's voice. "Buck, what's wrong?"

Buck spoke in amazement. "You're wearin' a dress!"

Ellie'd been so full of the events of the past evening that she'd forgotten about the dress and her reason for wearing it. She blushed shyly under Buck's unabashed stare. "I hope you like it."

Like it? Buck groaned inwardly. The soft lines of the Kelly green dress made Ellie look like a fashion model. Even in the dull light of the room, red and gold highlights danced in her auburn hair. But her eyes, there was something in them he'd never seen before. Maybe it was the color in the dress making them look so green. "Ellie, you look . . ."

The way Buck was looking at her made her nervous, so she decided to change the subject. "Buck, I have something to tell you."

Buck's heart sank. He figured she was dressed like this because she was leaving for Chicago . . . today. He braced himself for what she was going to say next. It was probably for the best anyway. He could learn to live without her, and it would make his life much easier to have her gone. "Ellie, you don't have to explain."

Ellie wasn't sure where to begin because now when she thought about what happened, the dream and its effect on her seemed so ridiculous. The direct approach seemed best. "Buck, I saw her."

Again Buck's mind raced ahead of Ellie's words as he tried to guess what she was talking about. "I don't understand. Who did you see?"

Ellie took a deep breath. "I saw your mother . . . in a dream. At least I think it was her. She was blond and so beautiful it took my breath away. I think she tried to tell me something. It all seems so crazy now. What do you think it means?"

Buck wasn't sure he'd heard right. He searched Ellie's face and inhaled deeply to see if he could smell alcohol on her breath. Nothing. His mind began to reel as he thought about the implications of what Ellie said. He'd heard the elders speak of dreams and visions, but he'd never given it much thought. "Ellie, I . . ."

"Time's up." The guard's unyielding expression made it plain there would be no exceptions.

Buck longed to reach out to her. "Ellie, there's so much I want to say."

"I know. I better go." Ellie stood up reluctantly. Her eyes brimmed with tears as she turned and walked away.

♦♦♦

Except for Ben, Tom and Ellie, the courtroom in Missoula was empty on Monday morning. Buck looked around the room when he was brought in by an attending officer. He smiled at Ellie as he walked by, and she tried to smile back bravely, but her heart was full of fear. There were too many "what ifs" involved for her to feel this situation was going to have a happy ending. They all stood as the judge entered. After he was seated, he spent several seconds studying the papers in front of him. Ellie began to fidget.

Finally, the judge peered over the top of his glasses at Buck. "Will Mr. Buck Eagle Plume please approach the bench?"

Buck got out of his chair and stood before the judge. A great sense of calm filled him. Somehow it no longer mattered to him what happened. He knew the Great Spirit was in control. He knew this was a test from which he would emerge stronger. He smiled inwardly, a sad smile, because this was what his grandfather had been trying to tell him all along. Buck wished his grandfather would walk through the

Buck and the Blue Roan

door to the courtroom so he could tell him he would be okay now.

Buck met the judge's gaze with quiet, steady eyes. "Good morning, Your Honor."

The judge's eyes widened in surprise. He wasn't used to courtesy from the people who came before him. He took a more measured look at the young cowboy with the strong face, and the clear, guileless eyes; the judge liked what he saw. He read the charges against Buck out loud.

After a few moments of silence in which everyone seemed to be holding their breath, he again addressed Buck. "Mr. Eagle Plume, because you live outside of the county, I cannot release you on your own recognizance. However, I will set your bail at one thousand dollars. If someone wants to post bond for you, you're free to go. Your trial will be in sixty days. I suggest you be there. Good day."

With Buck dismissed, Ben stepped forward to arrange for his release. Buck started to protest, but Ben silenced him. "You're the best hired hand I have. I can't let you fiddle around in jail when there's work to be done."

Buck took the big rancher's hand in his and shook it. "Thanks, Ben. You'll never know how much this means to me."

Tom stepped forward and gave his partner a hearty handshake. "Take care, kid. I've some things I have to look into here in town. I'll stop by the ranch to see you on my way home."

Buck studied Tom's face. His friend was up to something, and it worried him. He didn't need any more complications now. "Tom, take it easy. okay?"

Tom grinned mischievously. "Hey, 'easy' is my middle name. Don't worry. I know what I'm doin'."

Buck grinned. "That's what worries me."

With that, they left the courtroom. Buck was glad to be outside again, even if the city air smelled of exhaust fumes. It was better than the air inside the jail, and it was good to be with the people he cared about. "Can we go home now? I'm in need of some fresh mountain air."

The three of them got in Ben's pickup and headed south. Buck took in the scenery with new eyes. "We take this so much for granted. Maybe everyone should spend some time in jail. It's amazing how much it improves the vision."

Ben looked over at Buck. "I know what you're sayin', but no thanks. I'm getting' too old for that sort of eye opener."

They all chuckled, then lapsed into silence, each one contemplating Buck's words. Ellie's mind was far away when she felt Buck's strong hand take hers. She looked up and smiled into the warm brown eyes she had grown to love. Ben glanced over and saw the delicate fingers entwined with the strong ones of the young cowboy, and a knowing smile came to his lips.

♦♦♦

Tom was true to his word. Later that evening he stopped by the Magruder ranch and had a talk with Buck. They went to the cook shack. Buck stoked the fire in the old potbellied stove and brewed some coffee. He drew two chairs up to the stove and sat down, waiting. There was a silence for a few moments as Tom nursed his cup of coffee and gathered his thoughts. Finally, he spoke.

"I've been nosin' around to see what I could come up with on Eric Vance. We've only got sixty days to nail this guy. I don't know about you, but I figure the police need all the help they can get on this one. So far I haven't come up with much."

Buck smiled gratefully. "I figured you were playin' detective. I appreciate what you're doin', Tom."

"Hey, I don't want to lose my ropin' partner. I just hope we can come up with some evidence soon."

Buck looked discouraged. "I'm afraid I won't be much help. I can't leave the county. The saddle maker I was telling you about in Salmon might be able to help you. He knows every saddle maker in the West. This is cowboy country and a good place to move saddles. He may have had something come through his shop or know someone who has."

Tom nodded in agreement. "I'll look into it this week. We need all the help we can get. I'm going to talk to Gordon, too. He might have some ideas. In the meantime, don't worry. We'll get out of this . . . somehow."

Buck looked intently at Tom. "Have you ever thought maybe there's a purpose behind all this, and it may be my destiny to go to prison?"

Tom looked candidly at Buck. "I guess it comes down to a matter of trustin' your Maker, doesn't it?"

Buck sighed. "Yup."

◆◆◆

Ellie was emotionally and physically exhausted. Ever since Buck's arrest, her mind had been in turmoil. She tried to talk to Ben about her dream, but she could tell he was not able to relate to her experience. He nodded and smiled and tried to understand, but Ellie was sure he was just humoring her. He probably thought she was having some kind of emotional breakdown.

The scary part for Ellie was the thought that maybe she was, that what had happened was just the result of emotional stress. She needed to talk to someone who knew what she was feeling. It was Saturday. She dressed for riding and headed for the barn.

Ellie found Buck brushing the blue roan mare. She felt embarrassed, but desperate. "Are you going for a ride?"

Buck turned, and his expression brightened at the sight of her. "No, I'm waiting for my grandfather and Rusty. They're driving down to spend the day, so I'm sticking close by."

Ellie looked disappointed. "Oh, I didn't know. Uncle Ben didn't say anything about having company for lunch."

Buck pulled a stubborn tangle out of the mare's tail. "Grandfather didn't want to impose on Ben's hospitality, so we're going into Hamilton for lunch. Say, how would you like to come along with us?"

A bolt of hot anxiety shot through Ellie. Knowing what she now knew about Buck's family, she wasn't sure she could feel comfortable around them. "I don't think so, Buck. This should be a special time for you with your family. You haven't seen them for a long time."

Buck started to protest, but he was interrupted by the sound of a truck coming up the driveway. He waved to the occupants of the pickup and walked out to meet them.

Ed Eagle Plume got out first, nodded to Buck, then walked around to the passenger's side and opened the door. After his grandfather unfastened the seatbelt, Rusty jumped out of the truck and grabbed Buck in a huge bear hug. Buck rumpled his brother's hair, then took him by the hand and headed back to where he'd left Ellie standing. Ed Eagle Plume followed behind his grandsons as they headed back to the corrals.

Buck grinned broadly, obviously thrilled to see his brother. "Ellie, I want you to meet the most special person in my life, my brother, Rusty."

Ellie held back, feeling awkward. She hadn't known what to expect when Buck told her that Rusty was a victim of Fetal Alcohol Syndrome because she'd never seen anyone with that condition, and Buck had never mentioned Rusty's appearance. The young man standing before her had dark brown hair and eyes like his brother's, but all similarities stopped there. Rusty's head looked smaller than it should, and his eyes were small and slanted downward. His nose had practically no bridge to it, and his lower jaw and mouth seemed diminished in comparison to the rest of his face. She looked at the hand Rusty extended to her, a hand with bent, short fingers, and she tried not to pull back.

Gingerly she took the hand and cringed inwardly at the strange feel of it. "Hi, Rusty. Buck's told me all about you, and I'm glad to finally meet you."

Rusty shook Ellie's hand enthusiastically and grinned. "You pret
. . . ty. I li you."

Ellie blushed and pulled her hand gently from Rusty's grip. Before she could say anything, Rusty turned back to Buck. "Bu, you li her? She come home?"

Buck looked at Ellie and grinned sheepishly. "Ya, I like her, Rusty. Now let's go eat. I'm starving."

Rusty grabbed Ellie's hand. "El . . . lie come too."

This was more of a statement than a question, and Buck looked helplessly at his grandfather. Ed Eagle Plume patted Buck on the shoulder. "I think that's a great idea. Please come with us, Ellie."

Rusty didn't wait for Ellie's answer as he started back to the truck, tugging gently at her hand. She shrugged in resignation. "If it's okay with Buck."

Buck grinned at the sight of his brother leading Ellie back to the pickup. He looked at his grandfather. "Sure, why not."

Buck Evens the Score

THE WEEKS PASSED QUICKLY for Ellie. She wrote her mother to tell her she was planning on staying with Uncle Ben for a few more months. She didn't tell her why.

August slipped quietly into September. If possible, the mountain air was becoming clearer and fresher as the days grew colder. The cottonwoods and aspens along the Bitterroot River turned from green to bright yellow-gold almost overnight. Ellie found herself falling deeper and deeper in love with the valley. Would she ever leave it? Could she ever leave it? It was a question she couldn't bring herself to consider. Each day brought them closer to Buck's trial. Rumor had it the prosecuting attorney was building a strong case against him. Ellie knew one thing. She wouldn't leave until Buck's case was settled . . . one way or the other.

In spite of the beauty of the season, the past week had been depressing for everyone. Tom wasn't having any luck in his search for clues. After a long day, he was sharing his lack of news with Buck and Ellie in Ben's kitchen. I've got to hand it to Vance. He sure has covered his tracks. Nobody knows anything, or it they do, they're not sayin'."

Buck shook his head in dismay. "He's had to make a mistake somewhere along the line."

Tom sighed deeply. "Well, if he has, it isn't showin' up, and we're runnin' out of time."

Their grim thoughts were interrupted as Ben entered the kitchen.

"Excuse me while I get a cup of coffee. I can see by your cheerful faces Tom hasn't come up with anything."

The three friends remained silent. Ben continued. "Say, I hear there's a big jackpot ropin' at Hamilton this weekend. You fellas think you can still catch a steer?"

Buck and Tom exchanged glances. Buck looked at Ben and grinned. "With a little practice, we can catch anything on four legs. Let's do it."

After a few practice sessions, Buck and Tom were back to their usual form and looking forward to the weekend. Only Ellie had some doubts. She expressed them to Buck Friday night. "Buck, what if Eric Vance is there tomorrow? How can you stand to see him, knowing what he's doing to you?"

Buck smiled grimly. "It won't be easy, but I'm not going to let him ruin what's left of my time before the trial."

Ellie still wasn't convinced. "But what if he does something more to get you in trouble?"

"Hey, don't worry. If we all stick together, we can beat this thing. We can't give into fear about what might happen."

Ellie looked at Buck skeptically. "Do you really believe that?"

"I'd bet my life on it."

♦♦♦

They arrived at the rodeo grounds early because this was going to be a big roping. One hundred teams were signed up. It was an open roping with a three head for one hundred and fifty dollars. There was also a warm up roping with two head of steers for fifty dollars and a draw pot where ropers drew different partners from a hat. Buck warned Ellie the roping would take all day and might even run late into the evening.

The roping was late getting started. Ellie took note of the breeze and found a place to view the action upwind from the dust. Even though the arena was watered, it would dry out and get dusty later on. She enjoyed watching the first few teams compete.

When it was Buck and Tom's turn to rope, she found herself tensing up in excited anticipation. Tom backed his gray horse into the header's box. The horse stood quietly, just waiting. Buck had trouble with the blue mare. She shook her head in anger and refused to go into the heeler's box. Buck circled her twice, then tried again. This time he was successful.

For a moment everything seemed suspended in time. Ellie saw Tom nod his head; the chute clanged open, and the steer bolted out.

Buck grabbed the saddle horn and braced himself for the mare's powerful leap out of the roping box. She cleared the box and was hot on the heels of the steer. The mare positioned Buck for a good throw on the corner as Tom set the steer and turned off. Buck threw his loop and caught the steer's heels as they came off the ground. The mare buried her haunches in the ground and braced herself for the jerk of the rope as everything came tight. Tom's horse spun around the face of the steer, and the flagger dropped his flag, stopping the timer's clock. The announcer's voice came over the speaker telling their time, a six point two seconds run for Ford and Eagle Plume. Buck and Tom let out a victory yell and pumped their fists.

Ellie cheered and clapped, her heart pounding. She could imagine the thrill it must have been for Buck and Tom.

The rest of the first round of roping seemed to drag after their run. As the morning wore on towards noon, Ellie grew tired and hungry. She left her spot and headed for the parking lot. There was a thermos of coffee and sandwiches in Buck's truck. She hoped something in her stomach would perk her up. As she approached the truck, she turned red with anger. Parked next to Buck's rig was Eric Vance's van and horse trailer. Of all the nerve! She couldn't believe it. On the heels of her anger, fear crept in. What if Eric was in the van? She wanted to run back to the arena until she remembered Buck's words of the evening before. No, she would just ignore Mr. Vance. Why let someone like him ruin her day? Ellie set her jaw resolutely and headed for Buck's truck.

To her relief, nobody was around Eric's rig. She got in the truck and poured a cup of coffee and ate a sandwich, but instead of waking her up, it had the opposite effect. She decided to lie down for a quick nap. Her eyes closed, and she fell asleep,

The approaching sound of boots on gravel finally woke Ellie. She thought it was probably Buck and Tom coming to take a lunch break. She knew she would be in for some teasing and was about to sit up, ready with an excuse, when something about the voices caused her to stop. That was not Buck talking. It was Eric!

Ellie's heart began to pound, and her mouth went dry. She sank farther down on the seat. Ellie heard Eric open the sliding door to his van. He was talking to someone. There was a brief lull in the conversation punctuated by the snap-hiss of beer cans being opened

Eric began talking again. "I can't believe this. Eagle Plume is being real helpful. Wouldn't it be a shame if the police found more incriminating evidence on him, his being out on bail and all?"

The other man laughed wickedly. "You want me to 'borrow' someone's saddle and put it in his rig?"

"That sounds like a fine idea, and make it a new one. I've spotted a few that should bring a good price. We'll add those to the one we've got in back."

Ellie felt as though she would suffocate. *So, Eric really was the one stealing the saddles.* She would have to wait until he and his partner were gone, then she would go tell Buck and Tom what she'd overheard. Maybe they could catch Eric in the act of stealing one of the saddles.

The minutes ticked by slowly. Ellie hadn't heard anymore outside noise for a while, so she sat up cautiously and looked around. The truck door sounded too loud when she opened it. As she eased out of the truck and turned to close the door gently, her arm was caught in a painful grasp.

A man's ice cold voice spoke. "Going somewhere, Miss Parker?"

Ellie gasped and started to scream. Eric clasped his hand roughly over her mouth. She found the fleshy edge of it and bit down hard. Eric swore and pulling free, backhanded her across the mouth. The pain and shock of the blow took Ellie's breath away, and she felt blood trickle from the corner of her mouth.

Eric's partner soon had her legs, and she was thrown into the van. Once inside, the two men wasted no time putting a gag in her mouth and tying her hand and legs with a rope. When they were done, they sat back, breathing heavily. Eric's partner looked worried. "Now what are we gonna do? She was in that truck the whole time we were talkin'. She heard everything."

"Don't worry. Miss Parker's going to have to have an accident." Eric looked down at Ellie and caressed her cheek with the back of his hand. "What a pity to have to waste such a fine piece of flesh."

Ellie cringed under his intimate touch, and a paralyzing terror filled her whole being. Vance's partner spoke. "What kind of accident did you have in mind?"

Eric sneered down at Ellie. "It would be a shame if one of these spirited rope horses kicked Miss Parker in the head when she wasn't looking, now wouldn't it?"

Eric's partner grinned sadistically. "It sure would. You want me to do it now?"

"No. We need to mingle for a while first. I want lots of people to see us in the arena. You can take care of it during the draw pot roping. Things get confusing with everyone roping with a different partner."

The two men cross-tied Ellie between the rear door and the front seat. She couldn't scream or move enough to make any noise. She started to sob, but the gag in her mouth made her choke. These men were actually going to kill her! Fear and trembling took over her body and mind.

She called out in her mind. "Someone please help me!"

♦♦♦

Buck and Tom were pleased with their overall performance. They'd won the fast go and the average in the three for seventy-five roping, but they'd not done as well in the two for twenty-five, so they decided to enter the draw pot. It was getting to be a long day, and they were tired.

As they were leaving the arena, Buck turned to Tom. "Have you seen Ellie anywhere?"

Tom squinted his eyes to shut out the glare of the late afternoon sun and scanned the fence. "Come to think of it, I haven't. Of course, with all these people it's easy to get lost in the crowd."

"It's going to be a while before the draw pot starts, and we're pretty far down in the line-up. Let's give the horses a rest and grab a bite to eat. We can look for Ellie later."

The two cowboys rode back to Buck's rig. They both stopped their horses short when they saw Eric's van parked next to Buck's pickup. Tom shook his head in disgust. "Some people have a lot of nerve."

Buck's stomach knotted. "If I was a vengeful person, I'd be sorely tempted to let the air out of his tires . . . all of them."

Tom chuckled. "I know what you mean, but it takes a special kind of person to do a thing like that. I don't think you'd qualify for the 'creep of the year' award."

Buck and Tom tied their horses to the side of the trailer and loosened their cinches. When they were done, they went to the pickup for some coffee and a sandwich. Buck chuckled. "Well, it looks like Ellie's been here. She's put a sizeable dent in the sandwiches and coffee."

Tom grinned. "And I thought people are supposed to lose their appetites when they're in love."

♦♦♦

Ellie struggled for each breath. She was cramped, and the gag in her mouth choked her. The rope around her wrists had chafed them raw. The sound of approaching horses finally broke through her concentration. Her terror increased. Eric's partner must be coming back to bash in her head and throw her under some horse! The most agonizing thought was that he could probably get away with it.

She held her breath, waiting for the door of the van to open. The seconds ticked by painfully slow. When the door didn't open, Ellie let out her breath and strained her ears to listen. She could hear the sound of two men talking. A faint glimmer of hope began to glow deep within her. What if it was not Eric and his partner, but Buck and Tom instead?

Ellie tried to scream, but all she could do was gag. The rope she was cross-tied with bound her so tightly she couldn't move, yet she knew she must find a way. The men had stopped talking. Maybe they were leaving! More mentally than verbally Ellie cried out to Buck. She thrashed around, trying to make the van move, trying to make a noise of any kind until the ropes cut mercilessly into her flesh. Finally, in exhaustion, she passed out.

♦♦♦

Buck stopped in the middle of eating his second sandwich. He looked at Tom. "Did you hear something?"

Tom finished swallowing his food. "What did you have in mind? I'm hearin' lots of things."

Buck went quiet, straining his senses. "Shhh. I could've sworn I heard someone yelling, only it sounded far away. Something's wrong."

Tom looked at Buck skeptically. "Now don't go gettin' spooky on me. What do you mean, somethin's wrong?"

"I don't know. I just feel something. Ellie's in trouble." Buck opened the door and stepped out of the truck. As he did so, he thought he saw Eric's van moving. "Tom, look at this!"

Tom came around the front of the truck. "What's up?"

Buck pointed to the vehicle. "Watch the van. It's moving."

Tom looked at the van and then at Buck. "Man, you are going spooky. Now you're starting to see things."

Buck continued to watch the van, but nothing happened. He sighed and turned away. "Maybe you're right. Ellie's probably with Ben. Let's go find them."

They started to walk back to the arena. Suddenly, Buck stopped in his tracks. "I've got to see for myself."

Tom looked at him in disbelief. "Now what's botherin' you? Hey, what are you doin'?"

Buck walked back to the van and went to the side door. He knew he was taking a chance. He tried to look through the darkened windows, but he couldn't see. He knocked on the door. The van moved ever so slightly. He pounded on the door, then put his ear against it.

"Tom, I think I hear something." He ran around to the front of the van and grabbed a large rock.

Buck and the Blue Roan

Tom looked at him, shocked. "Are you out of your mind? If Eric sees you breaking into his van, it will be one more charge against you."

"I have, to know." With that, Buck shattered a side window. He reached through the jagged hole and unlocked the door. He turned the handle and slid the door open. "Ellie!"

In a matter of seconds, Buck and Tom cut Ellie's bonds. As soon as she was free, she threw her arms around Buck's neck and sobbed into his shoulder. Buck held her tight as the anger swelled in him. He could deal with Vance's attack against him. But his hurting Ellie was more than he could stand. He took hold of her shoulders and pushed her gently back. Buck grimaced at the sight of her bruised mouth and the raw rope burns on her wrists. "Ellie, tell me what happened."

In between sobs, Ellie poured out her story. "Buck, he was actually planning to kill me!"

Buck and Tom looked at each other in mutual understanding. Buck brushed the tears from Ellie's cheeks. "You get in the front seat of my truck. Lock the doors and lie down on the seat. Stay there. We'll send the paramedics over."

Ellie grabbed Buck's arm. "What are you going to do?"

Buck spoke with grim determination. "We're going huntin'."

Buck helped Ellie into the truck and made sure the doors were locked. He was reaching to get the rope off his saddle when Tom's voice stopped him short. "We've got company comin'."

The two of them hurried out of sight behind the van. They watched Eric's partner approaching. Tom signaled to Buck that he would circle around behind the man. Buck nodded and waited. By now he could hear the footsteps of Eric's partner and then the sound of the sliding door opening. There was a moment's silence, then the sound of cursing.

Buck stepped around the front of the van. "Are you lookin' for someone?"

Eric's partner froze for a second, stunned by Buck's sudden appearance. Then a look of cunning came to his face. He spun around and ran . . . straight into Tom, who caught him with a right uppercut to the jaw. The look on Tom's face would be the last thing he would remember until he regained consciousness.

The two cowboys made sure their prisoner was not going to go anywhere. They gagged and tied him and left him on the ground. Then they planned their next move.

Buck spoke first. "Tom, you call the sheriff and the medics. I'll tend to our friend, Mr. Vance."

Tom looked skeptical. "You sure you can handle him by yourself?"

Buck nodded. "I'm sure. Besides, I owe him one, and I'll have a whole arena full of ropers on my side."

Tom pulled the keys from the van ignition, put them in his pocket and grinned knowingly at Buck. "I'd hate to see Vance leave this party prematurely."

Buck and the Blue Roan

The two friends parted company, and Buck headed resolutely for the arena. He stopped outside the gate to check out the situation. He found out that Eric and the man he was roping with would be up after the next two steers out. Buck slipped unnoticed through the gate and walked over to where Gordon was sitting on his horse.

Buck spoke quietly. "I've got a snake to catch. Vance threatened to kill Ellie, and he's got a van full of stolen saddles. I'd appreciate your backup."

Gordon's expression never changed; his eyes just narrowed. "Why that dirty, low-down skunk. I'm with you all the way. I'll pass the word."

Buck left Gordon's side and approached Eric's horse. "Vance, get off your horse. I want to talk to you."

Eric smiled down condescendingly at Buck. "Well, if it isn't the jailbird. I'll stay on my horse if it's all the same to you."

With that, he dismissed Buck and turned to say something to the man next to him, but he never had a chance to finish his sentence. Buck reached up, grabbed Eric's belt and dragged him off his horse. The other ropers moved their horses back to give them room. All eyes were on the two antagonists. Buck and Vance circled each other, looking for a chance to strike. Buck had little to no experience fist fighting. He'd taken boxing in high school for P.E., but this was different. He knew, at best, he could only hope to keep Eric busy until the sheriff arrived.

From out of nowhere, a knife blade flashed in the growing dusk. Vance smirked at the shocked expression on his adversary's face. He moved in, forcing Buck to back up. So intent was he on cutting Buck, he didn't notice the horse and rider approaching him.

Just as Vance made a deadly lunge, Gordon threw a loop that settled down around Eric's waist, pinning his arms to his side. Gordon jerked his slack, dallied his rope and backed his horse. Eric hit the ground with a thud that knocked the wind out of him, and before he could move, Buck kicked the knife out of his hand. The siren of an approaching police cruiser wailed in the distance.

Buck grinned up at Gordon. "Thanks, friend!"

Gordon turned his head and spit a brown stream of tobacco juice into the arena dirt. A soft puff of dust rose where it hit the ground. The crow's feet at the corners of his blue eyes deepened with his grin. "Glad to oblige, Buck. I'll use a sorry excuse like Vance for a chance to throw a loop anytime."

♦♦♦

Ellie stepped out on the porch of the Magruder ranch house. Ben had gone to bed exhausted, but she was far from sleep. Her nerves were still on edge, so she sat down on the porch swing and looked up at the night sky. The evening was unbelievably clear, and each star shone with a special brilliance.

Her thoughts were interrupted by the sound of approaching footsteps. For a moment she panicked before she remembered where she was. The medication the doctor had given her hadn't helped relieve the fear she still felt, and she didn't think she could stand any more surprises. Ellie caught herself holding her breath until finally, a familiar form appeared out of the darkness.

"Buck?"

"Good evening, ma'am. I thought I better come up and see how you're doing." Buck climbed the porch steps.

It was good to hear the teasing back in Buck's voice. All of the pressure and emotion of the past few weeks came crashing down on Ellie. "Oh, Buck . . . !"

Buck held out his hand to her. "Come here."

Ellie went willingly into Buck's open arms. As he pulled her to him, relief flooded over her. The sheer strength of him gave her comfort. She rested her head against his chest and listened to the strong beating of his heart. The rhythmic sound soothed her raw nerves. Ellie felt Buck's warm breath on her hair as he bent down and gently touched his lips to her forehead. She looked up into his strong face, unashamed of her tears. "Buck, I love you so much!"

Buck's hold on her tightened before he released her. He took her face in his rough hands and brushed the tears away with his thumbs. "I've loved you ever since that first chicken dinner. I never had a girl try to kill me that way before. It was a different approach from what I'm used to, but it worked."

Ellie punched him playfully in the shoulder before she returned to his embrace. "You're such a cowboy."

Buck chuckled softly. "Now there's an oxymoron for you—a cowboy Indian. Which reminds me why I headed up here. Would you join me at a dance in St. Ignatius this weekend?"

Ellie smiled through her tears. "I'd love to."

CLOSING THE CIRCLE

ELLIE FELT SCARED and excited at the same time as she and Buck drove north into the Flathead valley. She had so many questions about Buck's family. A strained and awkward shyness rode between them in the truck. Ellie pretended to sleep; Buck turned on the radio and tapped his fingers on the steering wheel, keeping time with Alan Jackson's "Mercury Blues."

When they arrived in front of Buck's home, Ellie didn't have time to worry about the uneasiness. Rusty rushed to the pickup and opened the door. His face beamed with happiness.

Rusty grabbed Ellie's hand. "Hi, El . . . lie. Hi, Bu."

Ellie smiled at his enthusiasm and got out of the truck. Buck got out and came around to the passenger's side to give his brother a hug. Ed Eagle Plume hung back until Rusty finished with his welcome, then he stepped forward to greet Ellie. "I'm so glad you could join us for the weekend, Ellie. It's not the fanciest accommodations in the valley, but it's a friendly place."

Ellie shook her head. "I'm thrilled to be here, and I can hardly wait to go to the dance. I've seen country dancing on YouTube. It looks like fun, especially the line dancing."

Buck's grandfather shot him a questioning look. Buck grinned and shrugged his shoulders, but said nothing. The group headed up the walkway to the small weather-beaten house and were embraced by its warmth as soon as they entered.

Ellie inhaled deeply. "Mmmmm. What's that wonderful smell?"

Buck smiled at her response. "That's Sweetgrass burning. We use it for ceremonial cleansing and to give our home a sense of well-being. The smoke carries our prayers to the spirits."

Rusty continued to give Ellie the grand tour of the house while Buck and his grandfather did the evening chores. He showed her the buffalo head above the fireplace, the dream catcher in the kitchen window, and then he proudly showed her his room. The walls were covered with watercolor paintings of strange designs. Ellie pointed to them. "Who painted these?"

Rusty grinned and pointed to himself. "Me did."

Ellie squeezed his hand. "They're beautiful pictures, Rusty."

After finishing the chores, Buck and his grandfather sent Ellie to the living room while they fixed a venison steak and potato dinner. When it was time to eat, Buck found her dozing in the big chair in front of the fireplace. He shook her shoulder. "Hey, it's time to eat. We need to get going, or we'll miss the dance."

Everyone ate in relative silence as they savored the delicious meal. Ellie's nerves were on edge because she was afraid of making a fool of herself in front of Buck and his grandfather. The feeling grew as they washed and dried the dishes. The short ride into the countryside increased the tension she felt. She was surprised when Ed Eagle Plume pulled the truck to a stop in front of a plain wood-sided long building instead of a well-lit dance club. She chuckled nervously, and Buck looked at her questioningly. She spoke in answer to his look. "I guess I still have a lot to learn about Western living. I assumed we'd be dancing in a night club like we do in Chicago."

Once again Ed gave Buck a quizzical look over the top of Ellie's head. Buck just grinned. "Come on, Ellie. I think you're going to like this."

The four of them climbed out of the crowded pickup and entered the hall. Ellie stopped and stared. The big open room in front of her was full of Native Americans. Men and women lined the walls, sitting on folding chairs or standing while they talked with each other. Children of all sizes chased each other around the room. Several chairs circled the drums that occupied the center of the dance floor. Drummers and singers sat in the chairs.

The drum teams began to warm up, and some of them were adjusting the microphones nearby. Ellie blinked her eyes, thinking she was seeing things because many of the people in the room were dressed in ceremonial Native attire. Several men wore elaborate headdresses and feather bustles with colorful beadwork accenting breach cloths and breastplates. Most of the women wore cream or tan leather dresses decorated with beautiful bead work, and some wore or carried a traditional shawl.

Ellie grabbed Buck's arm. "Buck, what's going on here?"

Buck grinned innocently. "It's the dance I invited you to. Actually, it's much more than a dance; it's a powwow."

Ellie still looked confused. "What exactly is a powwow?"

Buck looked slowly around the room before answering. "The powwow is more than a social gathering; it's a symbol of renewal of our Native American identity. It reminds us who we are and where we come from. Here we honor our culture, our religion and our elders, but it's not exclusive to Native Americans. Everyone is welcome. And the most important thing about it is families have a fun time doing it."

As Buck explained the powwow to Ellie, Ed Eagle Plume stepped forward and spoke into a cordless microphone. He offered a prayer to the Four Directions, speaking in his native Salish language, and then he opened the powwow by announcing the Grand Entry. The first drum team started their rhythmic beat as they sang a traditional song.

All of the dancers moved out on the dance floor in a wave of color and motion that symbolized the harmony of the Flathead people. Ellie watched in awe, and her foot started to tap to the compelling beat of the drum. Buck noticed her reaction and smiled.

After the Grand Entry, the individual dances began with each drum team taking turns drumming and singing. The Fancy Dancers took to the floor first, starting out slowly, their bodies undulating to the rhythm of the song, and their moccasin covered feet keeping perfect time to the tempo of the drumbeat. Their porcupine roaches and eagle feather bustles bobbed with them. As the drummers reached a crescendo, the dancers kept up with the increased tempo, their bodies moving in a blur of action as each dancer competed for the prize. The dance ended with a resounding downbeat, which stopped the dancers as one.

The next dancers were the Grass Dancers, named for the long stands of yarn hanging from their yokes, shirtsleeves and leggings. As they danced, these strands moved like the tall grass on the prairie, adding their beauty to the pageantry of motion displayed by each individual. The women's shawl dance followed the Grass Dance. Each woman or girl moved to her private interpretation of the song, often spreading her shawl like the wings of the eagle as she twirled and danced. After these dances ended, Ed Eagle Plume invited everyone to participate in the traditional Owl Dance, a dance of welcome and universal fellowship.

Buck took Ellie's hand and headed for the dance floor. "Come on."

Ellie pulled back self-consciously. "Oh, no. I don't know how. I feel so out of place here."

Buck grinned at her and continued to guide her toward the dance. "That's what this is all about, making you feel welcome and a part of the powwow. Come on and try it. Where's the bad girl from Chicago?"

Ellie gave into Buck's appeal. He led her to a spot beside Rusty and his grandfather, who were in a group forming a large unbroken circle around the drum team. Rusty took Ellie's other hand as the drum team started the timeless Owl Dance. Ellie shuffled along as she tried to figure out the steps; it didn't take long. As she relaxed, the rhythmic beat worked its magic on her spirit and allowed her body to move comfortably with the music. The tension left her face, and she smiled warmly at Buck and Rusty. By the end of the evening Ellie participated in several communal dances, and Buck introduced her to many of his friends and their families. Finally, after everyone seemed worn out, the dancing stopped, and Ed Eagle Plume announced the giveaway.

Once more Ellie was full of questions. "Buck, what's going on?"

Buck looked with renewed pride and appreciation on his people. "This is a very important part of the powwow. We give gifts to honor our elders and to help those who are in need. Because we are all one, when one person hurts, we all hurt. We take care of each other, and we honor each other."

Tears welled up in Ellie's eyes. "I never knew, but I do feel an incredible love here. Thank you for letting me be a part of this."

Buck took Ellie's hand. "Grab your coat. I want you to see something."

Buck and the Blue Roan

Buck and Ellie went outside. The cold night air shocked their skin after being in the warm building. A full moon rose high in the sky over the Mission Mountains, creating a startling silhouette.

Ellie shivered slightly and moved closer to Buck. "I never knew anything could be so awesome."

Buck put his arms around Ellie and pulled her close. "Ellie, I love these mountains and this valley. And I love you."

Ellie opened her mouth to speak, but was silenced by Buck's warm lips on hers.

Buck gave her a hurt look. "Ellie, what's wrong?"

Tears brimmed in her eyes. "Buck, I love you, but I can't stay here. Summer's over. I've got to go back to Chicago. I've got to try to get my high school diploma or a G.E.D . . . and my mom needs me. Buck, I've really hurt her. I need to make it up to her somehow.

Buck pulled her back to his chest. He put his face into her rich auburn hair and inhaled deeply, not wanting to let the moment go, but knowing he must. "Ellie, I understand, but I will come for you. In the spring I will come. I promise."

◆◆◆

Even though it was almost one o'clock in the morning when the Eagle Plumes returned home, Buck crawled out of bed at six a.m. to go do chores for his grandfather. The crisp morning air reminded him that snow would soon be covering the ground again. He broke the thin layer of ice on the water trough before he took grain to the steers. They stood against the far side of the corral and eyed him suspiciously, the steam rising from their nostrils. As soon as Buck moved away, they came running and bucking to the feeder and plowed their noses into the grain while their long tongues scooped the feed into their mouths. Buck grinned at their enthusiasm.

As he leaned against the top rail of the fence, he looked out across the pasture to the lone cottonwood tree that stood sentinel over Chester's grave. That cold March day seemed like a lifetime ago. So much had changed; he had changed. Tears stung Buck's eyes as memories of the buckskin gelding played gently through his mind.

A strong hand on his shoulder caused him to look around. "Grandfather!"

Ed Eagle Plume followed Buck's gaze. "He was a great horse. You'll probably never find another one to equal him, but they all have their good points."

Buck swallowed his emotions. "I know, but I still miss him."

A nicker from the nearby horse corral drew Buck's attention. The blue roan mare nickered again and moved closer to the fence. Buck walked over to her and stroked her neck through the corral poles. The brown gelding stood behind her.

"Well, Miss Kitty, welcome home. You've earned this." Buck unlatched the gate and pulled it open. For a brief moment the blue roan hesitated, then she exploded out of the gate, racing across the pasture. The brown gelding followed her, bucking and kicking with joy.

The two men watched the horses as they raced around the pasture. Finally, they stopped near the old cottonwood tree and dropped their heads to graze.

Ed cleared his throat. "With you gone, I've done a lot of thinking this summer. I owe you an apology, Buck. It seems all the time I was trying to protect you, I was really hurting you. I never meant to push you away."

Buck turned to face his grandfather. "Grandfather, all I ever wanted was for us to be a family. I miss Mom and Dad so much, and I guess I didn't want to understand what was really going on with you. I'm ready now, and I need to know. Tell me everything about Vietnam . . . please."

As the two men walked across the pasture and sat down on a log next to the old cottonwood, the morning sun broke over the craggy rim of the Mission mountains and flooded the Flathead valley with warmth. A shaft of sunlight filtered through the Dream Catcher hanging in the living room window, spreading its reflection across the back of the old chair and gently kissing the tiny picture on the table next to it of a pretty blond woman with two little boys standing next to a tall Native man in a military uniform.

About the Author

Stormy Kurtz was born in central Montana. She grew up on her parents' ranch in the Paradise Valley located near Yellowstone National Park. Her young adult years were immersed in ranch and rodeo culture. She later attended the University of Montana where she earned a Bachelor of Arts degree in Secondary Education with an emphasis on English and Journalism. After moving to Spokane, WA, she raised her two sons, Buck and Skyler, as a stay-at-home mom. Eventually, she returned to college to earn a Master's degree in Literature. Stormy has enjoyed teaching English for 20 years at Spokane Falls Community College. She currently lives with her husband, Ron, on a small farm near Cheney, Washington, with their two horses, 25 chickens and one cat.